C000182369

Waldorf

Grenville Williams

FOURTH ESTATE • *London*

First published in Great Britain in 1997 by
Fourth Estate Limited
6 Salem Road
London W2 4BU

Copyright © 1997 by Grenville Williams

1 3 5 7 9 10 8 6 4 2

The right of Grenville Williams to be identified as the author of this work has been asserted by him in accordance with the Copyright, Designs and Patents Act 1988.

A catalogue record for this book is available from the British Library.

ISBN 1–85702–607–1

All rights reserved. No part of this publication may be reproduced, transmitted, or stored in a retrieval system, in any form or by any means, without permission in writing from Fourth Estate Limited.

Typeset by Palimpsest Book Production Limited,
Polmont, Stirlingshire
Printed in Great Britain by Clays Ltd, St Ives plc,
Bungay, Suffolk.

To my wife Mary, for putting up with my weird sense of humour for all these years, and to Joe Lane, my neighbour, whose loaded innuendos drove me on.

Chapter One

Reginald Bagshott-Hawkes (Capt.) Rtd stalked into the lounge carrying *The Times,* stopped, and cast a baleful eye at Waldorf, who was snoozing peacefully in his, Reggie's, favourite armchair. At least, Waldorf appeared to be snoozing. In reality he was wide awake and when he heard his master enter the room he lay there, with his eyes closed tight, waiting for the dreaded words.

'Out of that damned chair this instant.' No 'please' or 'thank you' or 'if you would be so kind . . .'

'Out, I say,' accompanied by a whack with *The Times* so that Waldorf shot out of the chair and headed for his basket in the conservatory, with drooping tail and lowered head, casting wary glances behind. The basket had been bought when his mistress brought him home as a tiny pup. Even though allowance had been made for growth, he had far surpassed their expectations and now slept half in and half out of it with either his head or his rear supported on old cast-off cushions. He looked part Irish wolfhound and part retriever, with the wolfhound predominant. His eyes were liquid brown and his greyish hair, on the long side, was now going a little white around the muzzle. As he lay there with his head hanging out of the basket, he could see Reggie in the lounge, slapping at dog hairs with his newspaper and muttering to himself. 'Damned dog . . . Should be outside . . . Like a blasted carthorse about the place,' etc, etc.

At last, when Reggie was finally satisfied that there were no dog hairs left on the chair, he sat down, shaking out his paper and giving one last glower in Waldorf's direction before beginning to read.

Reginald Bagshott-Hawkes was in his mid forties. He was bald-headed, with the remnants of hair growing at the sides carefully combed over the pate and held in place by judicious use of his wife Lucy's hair spray. A closely clipped moustache helped to maintain the military appearance he affected and he was given to wearing khaki shirts and drill trousers, together with highly polished brown shoes. Whilst at home, 'off duty' as he was wont to put it, he wore a carefully knotted cravat, but at the office he sported ties of one sort or another, quite often knitted.

He had been of undoubtedly smart appearance in his youth, but the effect was now spoiled by his body having run to fat and since he was only five foot eight inches in height what, in his youth, had been a broad compact figure now loomed large. He had been a captain in the army and something of a martinet but, since retiring from military life two years earlier, he had run a branch office of Wharfman's Insurance Brokers in Merton Stow, with recognised ability. Whilst he was respected there, few regarded him with affection. He was good at what he did, had a phenomenal memory; almost photographic, knew all the underwriting instructions of all the companies with which he dealt, and was able to recognise, instantly, faulty write-ups and other mistakes. The miscreant would be hauled up before him, given a good dressing-down and warned as to what would happen if there was not a significant improvement in his or her work.

Excuses were not accepted. It was all black and white with Reggie.

Those who had met his wife Lucy were amazed. She was his antithesis. Warm. Outgoing. Informally friendly. Where he would bark an order, she would ask nicely. He was all sharp corners and unbending; she was resilient and receptive. Whilst people around them wondered about their relationship, to them it was simple. He worshipped her and he was the love of her life. For all his abruptness and authority at the office, at home it was Lucy who ran things. She was subtle. She was manipulative. The seeds of some of his best ideas had been sown by Lucy. He often wondered why the office didn't run like clockwork as it appeared to him that his home did and put it down, wrongly, to an unwillingness on the part of his staff to accept an order without question.

It was Saturday morning, Reggie's favourite part of the week. The office didn't open on Saturdays, so he and Lucy had established a relaxed breakfast routine. Lucy would come into the dining room pushing the hostess trolley. Reggie would get out of his chair and help her to her seat. He was all old-world courtesy in his treatment of his wife and, before seating himself opposite her, would go into the kitchen to fetch the coffee percolator which he plugged in.

He loved Saturday mornings. The leisurely breakfast. Discussion of the morning papers. The trolley helped. No need for someone to keep getting up and down. Everything to hand. What was supposed to be hot was hot. Bacon, eggs, grilled kidneys, mushrooms, hot French rolls on which the butter melted. Heaven.

Breakfast over, he would clear away and load up the dishwasher, and whilst he waited for Lucy he would get the car out and give it a quick rub over with a duster so he'd be ready to start off when she came out. On going back to the house to check that everything that had to be shut off was shut off, he would turn to close and lock the front door and shout at Waldorf, 'Now you stay there, in that basket, and look after the place.' Of course, he was whistling in the wind.

'I'll bet anything that I'm not out of the drive before that damned dog is in my chair,' he would grunt to no one in particular as he got into the car and drove off.

He was right, of course. Well, almost. Waldorf waited for a good ten seconds after the sound of the car had completely faded away before he lumbered out of his basket and ensconced himself once more in his, Waldorf's, favourite armchair and fell fast asleep.

Reggie and Lucy's Saturdays followed a familiar pattern. A little shopping followed by a drive to a pub, usually to meet a couple of friends, and then an unhurried lunch, perhaps a stroll afterwards, and finally home. Sometimes they would go out to see friends for an evening, sometimes they would have people in. Over the years, their friends had become used to Reggie. The more astute among them saw him for what he was, a man who needed rules and regulations for himself. Left to his own devices he tended to be rather insecure, but with a rule book in his hand he was a match for anyone.

Most of them now knew how to joke with Reggie. Plain, straightforward jokes, no double meanings that left Reggie struggling to see what it was that everybody was laughing at; and no sex jokes. Even the more gentle ones such as what the actress said to the bishop left him squirming in confusion; and the night when Peregrine, his rather vulgar brother-in-law, had told the one about the nun who thought Bonking was a town in China almost scarred him for life. The chuckles that greeted that joke had been followed by screeches of laughter at Reggie's discomfort.

Reggie had been celibate until he married fifteen

years ago, and his very awkwardness and embarrassment had endeared him to Lucy. Sex had never been a subject of amusement to him.

Lucy had never seen Reggie naked. All their lovemaking was done in the dark. Lucy often wondered to herself what on earth he would be like if he had to go into hospital and use bed pans and be given bed baths. It was probably something to do with his childhood, but she would never know as he was an only child and his parents had passed on a few years before she and Reggie met. Reggie was loath to discuss his upbringing with her or anyone else. It didn't bother her a great deal, and it didn't seem to bother Reggie, so she judged it to be a harmless foible on his part and accepted it as such.

During the rest of the week, Reggie and Lucy lived a quiet life. There would be no visitors and they would generally have the evening to themselves. A night in. Reggie would watch the news on the box, then take Waldorf for a short walk, drop into the local for a brief visit then home to bed.

The landlord of the pub was an ex-army man as well. Not ex-officer, but ex-sergeant-major, some ten years older than Reggie. A man who had risen through the ranks and with whom he felt at ease. Ex-Sergeant-Major Davies was always smart, always in command of his pub. It was always 'Evening, Sir' when Reggie walked into the pub and there was never any need to order. Reggie's gin and tonic was on the bar almost as soon as he arrived. If it was quiet, Davies would stay with him, talking cricket or rugby or whatever, depending on the season or the craze of the moment. Oddly enough, the army was hardly ever mentioned. Theirs had not been a common experience. The only sure topics of conversation were sport and mutual acquaintances.

Sometimes Lucy came with him to the pub, and then they went into the lounge and Mrs Davies would come over and chat for a while. Lucy was well known in the community, the local 'big wheel': secretary of the WI; a meals on wheels volunteer; and so on, so no matter where she went, she was recognised.

Reggie had become used to being introduced as 'Lucy's husband Reggie', and as a result had become almost as well known as his wife. He was well aware that when he was at the office his house was, quite often, full of women, having a coffee morning; or a committee meeting or something or other for fallen women or orphans; or a protest meeting against any sort of industrial or local council mayhem that was going to change the size and character of Merton Minor.

He was in agreement with most of their aims, but the little sub-committees that were set up to organise trips to theatres and other venues often left him wondering why Lucy didn't delegate the job to someone else. It never dawned on Reggie that the essence of it all was the socialising that went with it. Contented with his limited social life, he had no desire to make new friends.

'These women annoy me,' he said to himself on more than one occasion. 'The trouble with most of them is that they've got nothing better to do. Ought to get themselves a job, or should be home, looking after their husbands more.'

Lucy had inner strengths. The eldest of a family of six, she was imbued with qualities of leadership, patience and a resilience that overcame most of the obstacles that life cast in her path. She was aware that she often took on too much but she also knew that she was the catalyst that turned the social wheel of the village. She had time for everybody.

A friend had asked, 'Lucy, how on earth do you manage to get on so well with that horrible old man Grayling? Don't know how you stand him.'

'It's easy enough,' said Lucy with a smile. 'I try to find something likable about him and go on from there. Everybody has something good buried in them somewhere. I just persevere until I find it.'

'You must be a saint.'

'Not really,' said Lucy, 'I get my off days too, you know.'

And so she did. Those were the days when she would phone her best friend Dulcie Nicholas, the doctor's wife, and they would drive off to Merton Stow or Swiffield or even Hungerford and shop and browse and have a leisurely lunch before driving back to Merton Minor, feeling fit to get on with life once more.

In response to his wife's preoccupation with village affairs, Reggie had developed a hobby of his own which now filled one side of his study with reference books. The army. From uniforms to regiments, battles to ceremonies. Biographies and autobiographies. Anything and everything to do with man's belligerence to his fellow man. It was not because he was belligerent himself that he delved. It was more out of curiosity. When he himself had been in the army, as orders came down from on high he had obeyed them without question. But ever since leaving military life, doubts had come unbidden into his head, and he had bought the odd book to try to get a picture of what went on in the minds of the people who led countries or factions or downright armed opposition.

He spent a great deal of time in his study. He found television mostly a bore, although he did like the odd documentary and the news. Sometimes, if there was something said on the box that he didn't agree with, he would turn to Lucy and castigate the individual concerned.

'Just listen to that fool. You can tell he hasn't roughed it. Always on the side of the great unwashed,' and a blast of a letter would go winging its way to the local press. Lucy would shake her head and smile. He was not one to suffer fools gladly, but his bark was worse than his bite.

His other recreation was gardening. No, not recreation, because it had to be done on a regular basis out of necessity. He and Lucy lived in a large detached house with a small garden at the front, and a huge one at the back. At the side of the house was a driveway leading to a fairly substantial garage that acted as a workshop, garden shed and store.

Over the years Reggie had gradually replaced the lawn at the back with coloured paving slabs and the large borders with four small, raised plots, each about four foot by twelve, which he found more easily manageable. As he liked to tell people, 'I could now do almost all of my gardening with a hoe, a brush and a hosepipe.' Trimmed hedges ran all around the property and a large water butt collected the run-off rain water from the garage roof.

On sunny evenings and weekends out came the sun loungers and patio set and some meals were taken 'al fresco'. Reggie was not too comfortable with that way of life and usually his sole concession to the weather was to remove his jacket and roll up his shirt sleeves, whilst Lucy sat in her bathing costume, soaking up the sun. Wearing a bathing costume was something that Reggie just did not do.

He hadn't been swimming since he was a child, except during his training days in the army, and he was well aware that he was nowhere near as attractive as he had been at that time. He also knew that he was extremely overweight and that he should diet and take more exercise, but he cringed at the thought of going to the local gymnasium.

Lucy never made any outright remarks about his size, but now and again she brought out some of his old clothes that he had had to discard as he gained weight and innocently asked him to 'Try this one on, Reggie, you used to look so nice in it,' then gave a little 'tut' as he struggled to do up the buttons and belts. Only his walks with Waldorf stopped him from ballooning into a real elephant of a man. He kept telling himself that he would definitely start his diet/exercise tomorrow, but procrastinated so that tomorrow never came.

Their next-door neighbours on either side were quite some distance away, so that there was an air of seclusion about the garden. The only time they were overlooked was when Jason, their next-door neighbours' small son, played in the little tree house that his father had built for him, but that wasn't very often.

On the other side, Mr and Mrs Kite were childless. 'Her choice, no doubt,' thought Reggie who, on the few occasions he'd been in their house, had thought how like a museum it was. A very modern museum, mind you, with not a thing out of place. 'No dog hairs here,' he'd mused. 'It's like one of those modern furniture warehouses, where the rooms are laid out with their own immaculate but impersonal new fittings.'

Immediately at the back of Reggie's house lived

the Taits, Myra and Stan. She was a big woman with the ability to transfix, with a glare, any hapless male who happened to offend her, whether intentionally or not. Stan on the other hand was of a retiring nature. Small of stature and grey: grey in manner and grey in appearance. And fussy. He reminded Reggie of a small tugboat fussing around a cruiser when he was out and about with Myra.

They owned a small, snappy pug dog that liked to sneak through a weak spot in the fence at the bottom of Reggie's garden and make a nuisance of himself with Waldorf. If Waldorf, in good weather, was tied up to his big kennel by the garage, Pug would come through and bark and snarl and skirt around the bigger dog as if trying to tempt him into making an attack. Waldorf would watch him from under lowered lids, in much the same way that he watched Reggie advancing on his armchair, and in the end Pug would stalk off, giving little yaps as if to say, 'Well, I taught that big bozo a lesson.' Easy-going old Waldorf would let him go.

Waldorf always wore a slip chain instead of a collar, and when he was tied up at the garage, it was to a length of chain with a spring clip at the end that attached to the chain around his neck. The other end was fastened to a ring cemented into the brickwork of the garage. Waldorf wasn't chained to the garage that often, mostly only when visitors were expected and dog hairs were unwelcome. So it was normally out with Waldorf and in with the Hoover before visitors arrived. He was such a placid old thing that he hardly ever protested, and some of the visitors went out of their way to go out to talk to him and take special titbits, all of which he accepted as his due. He would 'shake hands' when asked and roll over, but that was his lot, and no amount of training or bribing could make him perform any more complicated tricks.

Admittedly, if someone scratched his stomach, he would lie down and raise one paw in the air. But Reggie didn't think that was much of a trick. He knew a lot of people who would roll over and hold their hands in the air if they were having their stomachs scratched.

Privately Reggie thought that Waldorf was a bit thick, even though he did look intelligent. He'd seen some animal acts on television and had watched guide dogs for the blind being trained and he concluded that as a guide dog Waldorf would have been a disaster. 'He'd be the one needing a guide,' was his verdict.

He sometimes wished that Lucy had chosen a different type of dog. One who appreciated his luck in being chosen to live in luxury for the rest of his days. A dog who fawned on his owners, not one who, when he saw you, gave a single half-hearted wag of his tail and never came bounding down the drive as if you'd been away for years, as other dogs did. A dog that would give that Pug from over the back a good sending off, not let him walk all over the garden as if it were his own.

It was only when Reggie and Waldorf went for their evening walks that they seemed to suit each other. Reggie would let Waldorf off the leash and the dog would bound away to roam the hedgerows and course up as far as the wood. One short whistle from Reggie was all that was necessary to bring him back to heel, and one word would make him stay in that position as they walked back to the pub.

At the pub, Waldorf would revert to type. He would lie under the bench at the end of the bar, by a radiator in the winter, out of the way of people's feet, with his chin on his paws, eyes half open until a call from Reggie, 'Come on Waldorf,' brought him to his feet with a lurch and he would follow Reggie out with an air of resignation for the short walk home.

'Waldorf,' Reggie had mused, just a few nights ago. 'What a name for a dog.' It made no difference to Waldorf himself, but it prompted a few smiles when people heard it for the first time, and the reaction made Reggie cringe.

'He could have been called Hector or Hero or anything at all,' thought Reggie. 'Why did it have to be Waldorf?' It was the fault of Lucy's brother Peregrine – 'a bit of a poser,' Reggie thought – who had first used the name when the dog was brought home as a very good-looking puppy. He had been visiting them on his return from a 'sabbatical' to the United States and in talking about his visit had mentioned staying at the Waldorf Astoria. 'A throw-away line,' Reggie recalled sourly. At the sound of the word Waldorf the puppy, which had been sleeping on the floor, had for some unknown reason raised his head and wagged his tail, whereupon Peregrine had said it again and obtained the same reaction. That was that. Waldorf he became. A name with connotations of sophistication, of glamour – not at all appropriate to the bundle of grey rags Waldorf so closely resembled.

The only time Waldorf became powerfully animated was when his food – biscuits and Meaty Chunks – were put down for him and the call went up: 'Waldorf, dinner!' Then a great grey flash would come bounding up and almost devour the old tin dinner plate as well as everything on it.

Reggie's walks with Waldorf had originally been undertaken with bad grace, but, as time went by, he had in spite of himself begun to enjoy them. There were still some things, however, with which he found it hard to come to terms, and one of these was a dog's general habit of cocking his leg. At the first sight of a lamp-post, Reggie would drag Waldorf as far away from it as he could get him, within reason, until they arrived somewhere where there were no spectators. Only then was poor old Waldorf allowed to answer the call of nature, out of sight of prying eyes, so saving Reggie's finer feelings.

On the odd occasion when Waldorf caught Reggie out, he would stand with the lead in his hand trying to look as though Waldorf wasn't with him, a look of martyrdom on his face, and Waldorf would hardly be given time to finish what he was doing before being hauled off by his master, whose face would be scarlet with embarrassment.

One would think that, as someone who had spent many years in the army, all prudishness would long ago have been knocked out of him, but it hadn't happened in Reggie's case. He was aware that he was a little bit odd in this respect, but he couldn't seem to do much about it. He was just as embarrassed by his own private functions: if he had to use any of the town's toilets, he would bypass the stalls in favour of one of the cubicles and close the door, emerging fully buttoned or zipped up, hurrying out with downcast eyes.

Although it might not have been apparent to those around him, Reggie was aware of his shortcomings. He was a proper old 'stick in the mud', he thought to himself on more than one occasion. Sometimes he became frustrated with himself because he hadn't made more of a success out of life, but that didn't last long when he looked around him and saw that really, life was a gamble. On your way through it you passed lots of doors. You picked the one you fancied and went where it led you, to other doors and other choices. He had taken an army commission to 'see something of the world' and instead had seen the inside of various offices up and down the country and had become what was known as an 'office wallah'. Wrong door . . . or was it?

On leaving the army he had found it easy to get a job and easy to hang on to it. But now and again came the odd craving for something else. Something a little more glamorous; a little more adventurous. Something to crack the glaze of sameness that gets to everybody now and again.

On the whole, though, life was good to the Bagshott-Hawkes. Nothing disturbed the even tenor of their ways. Their likes and dislikes, happinesses and griefs were no more and no less than those of most people living. Sometimes a little ennui crept into Reggie's consciousness, but only occasionally. Earthquakes only happened in foreign countries.

Chapter Two

It began with Daft Jim.

Reggie had known 'Daft' Jim Contrell since he started courting Lucy eighteen years previously. The Contrells had lived in the village all their lives. They were one of the old, original families, the sort that called people who had only lived there twenty years or so 'newcomers'. Besides father Albert and mother Sophia there was Len, the eldest boy, his two sisters Stella and Amy, and Jim, the youngest. Nobody had realised that Jim was in any way abnormal until he was eighteen months old and it was a devastating discovery for all the family. He could not be left on his own for an instant, he wasn't potty trained until he was four and even that was above the expectations of the health visitor. He did learn things, but very slowly and more by hard experience than anything else. He had had to be shown that 'hot' meant 'don't touch or you'll get hurt', and gradually they had turned the word 'Hot' into 'Not' so that when he was finally allowed into the field behind the house the gate was touched and 'Not' shouted at him to make certain that he wouldn't attempt to open it and escape.

Of course, there were accidents galore. He had once drunk a bottle of whisky and been rushed to hospital to have his stomach pumped. There were now no locks on the toilet since the time he locked himself in and they had to have the door broken down to get him out; and all Len's tools had to be kept under lock and key.

It had seemed to take him four years to acquire the expertise that most humans achieve in one, and when he reached the age of ten that seemed to be that as far as his development was concerned. The worry in the family was what was going to happen to Jim when they either grew too old to look after him or passed away.

Physically, Jim had grown in a normal fashion. He was quite muscular but he couldn't run as fast as most boys his age because his coordination was awry. He was forever tripping over and grazing his knees and elbows.

'I don't know, Mam,' said Len after one incident when Jim tripped as he ran into the house and knocked over the fully laden tea table, trashing everything on it. 'I really don't know, but it might be better if we could get him into a home of some kind.'

'You're only saying that, Len, because you're mad at him at the moment. Now come on. You'd be the first to stick up for him if somebody else said that. He didn't mean it. Any more of those big sticking plasters in that box?'

Life at the Contrells' revolved around Jim. The girls had married and fled the nest, Albert had been killed by a bull some six years previously; a case of familiarity breeding contempt – he had turned his back once too often. Now only Sophia and Len were left to look after Jim, who had matured into a full-grown man with a mental age somewhere between eight and eleven and a very trusting nature. He could be left to wash himself, but that meant the whole bathroom being washed at the same time. Then he had to have his hair brushed and combed and he was checked over to see that he was as presentable as possible.

'He could,' thought Len on more than one occasion as he was brushing Jim's hair, 'have been a real good-looking bloke. All the girls would have gone for him.' And he was right. Jim would have been a handsome man if things had run differently. Blond. Blue eyes. Nice, regular features. Good teeth.

Len had come to accept that it had fallen to him to be Jim's mentor and it had so coloured his life that he had stopped courting. There was also a niggling doubt at the back of his mind that he might be carrying the same fault that had made Jim the way he was, and he didn't feel that he could chance having kids himself.

And so it might have continued if life ran along rails like a train, and not like a roller-coaster.

On Friday night, the ninth of October 1987, the

pub had a carnival air about it. Daft Jim was in the bar when Reggie and Waldorf arrived after their customary walk. He was usually only allowed two shandies otherwise he became quite uncontrollable, but tonight was different. Something had *happened* to Daft Jim.

He had, Reggie was told, walked into the pub like any normal person. Gone was the vacant grin that had been a perpetual feature of his face. He had greeted the regulars by name in an ordinary person's voice and had asked one or two, who were generally kind to him, if they wanted a drink. They, bemused by his different appearance, had accepted.

After a while he had joined in the general conversation and had astounded regulars with his knowledge of every subject that was broached. He was still dressed in the ill-fitting clothes that he normally wore, but they were now buttoned up, with each button in its proper hole. His lips no longer hung loose and dribbled and his hair was properly groomed.

'You want to listen to this, sir,' said Davies as he served Reggie his gin and tonic. 'A most puzzling thing.'

He moved back along the counter, motioning for Reggie to follow. Reggie waved his drink to Len Contrell as he joined them and Davies said, 'Start again, Len, from the beginning.' Len obliged.

'Now you know that Jim has never been anywhere on his own. It's either been me or one or another of the family, or a friend that takes him out. Or maybe one of the more responsible kids from the village takes him down to the shop for sweets or crisps. When I say that he never goes out on his own, I mean into the street or the village. He could be a danger to himself if a car came along. He isn't able, or rather, *wasn't* able, to cope with the traffic. He used to go out of the back of the house into the field and up as far as the wood, but he would never go into the wood on his own. He was frightened of it, just like a young kid would be. So we never had any worries about him going out there as there was no way out of the field except through our back door and back gate or the gate right alongside our cottage.

'Well, yesterday afternoon he went out of the back gate into the field at about four o'clock to watch some rabbits that he said he saw from his bedroom window: bunny rabbits he called them. We thought nothing of it, but when we went out to call him for his tea, he wasn't there. We searched high and low and couldn't find him. We called the police and the welfare people but not a sign of him. We were worried sick. We looked in the pond, but it's only inches deep and he would have stuck up like a sore thumb if he had been in there. We searched the woods and it's a funny thing, but the dogs wouldn't go in there and we thought that was suspicious in itself, so we searched it even more thoroughly, but there was no sign of him. We'd phoned my sisters and they came over with their husbands. We were up all night, so we were exhausted, and I was making a cup of tea for all of us in the kitchen when we heard the front door open and in he walks, as cool as a cucumber, and says, "Good morning," as if it was the most natural thing in the world to vanish for sixteen hours without a trace. We all started shouting at him at once, but suddenly we went quiet because we realised that he was different. I mean he was normal. I don't mean normal in the sense that he was normal as usual, but that he was "normal" like us. He looked at us . . . no . . . he *examined* us with a sort of amusement. We were all standing there looking at him and he went over and got his mug, the one with the bunny rabbits on, and he made himself a cup of tea. . . . *A cup of tea!* . . . He picked up the teapot and we all shouted "Hot" and he turned and grinned at us and we felt such fools, because the intelligence was shining out of his eyes.

'You remember what he was like when you looked at him, sir, a sort of vacant look. What a difference! I don't know if I can make you appreciate how we felt. Mother was the first to move. She was across the room and had him in a bear hug, with the tears streaming down her face. He put his arms around her and stroked her hair murmuring, "There, there," and we were all so shocked that we couldn't start talking or asking him questions for a while. Then we all started talking at once.'

Len stopped, his face working with remembered

emotion. Reggie gestured towards Len's empty glass to Davies, who refilled it and put it back on the bar. Len accepted it gratefully and took a pull at it before continuing.

'We asked him where he'd been, but he couldn't remember anything that had happened after he walked out of the house yesterday afternoon, until he "came to", as it were, walking through the gate at High Tor on the way back down the lane to the village. He realised that he felt different, and he sat on a stile for about half an hour coming to terms with his new intelligence. He said that he had tried to remember what had happened. He didn't know how long he had been "out of life", as he put it, but he had gone into the paper shop before he came home and bought a paper on tick – he never carried any money, and he was used to getting things like sweets and chocolate on tick if he went to the shop with one of the kids, so there was nothing strange in that, except that that was the first time he'd ever bought a newspaper. No one could remember him ever being up that early in the morning before. He read the date on the paper – we didn't even know that he could read – and saw that there was only a day gone by, but whatever had happened, he was grateful. He knew that now he was "normal", but there was still something niggling him at the back of his brain. He said that it wasn't serious, and whatever it was would come to him.' Len stopped again, and they all turned to look at

Jim, talking and laughing animatedly with four or five regulars.

Reggie looked on with a tinge of scepticism. He tended to regard most of the mentally ill as malingerers. They were putting it on. They didn't want to understand so they didn't even try. He said, more for something to say than for anything else, 'Has he seen a doctor?'

Len shook his head. 'No, not yet. He'll have to see him though. Old Dr Simmons will have a fit himself when he sees what he's like now. We can't understand it. We were told that he would never be normal. That he had reached the limit of any improvement. He never had any proper schooling except for the special schools, and suddenly here he is, better informed than any of us. It doesn't make sense. Ask him anything you like, he'll know the answer. He's better than a computer: spelling, arithmetic, history, anything.' Len shook his head in wonderment.

Reggie turned back to the bar and winked at Davies to show his disbelief, shaking his head slightly. Of course, there was certainly an improvement there, that was obvious, but this accolade of genius . . . He shook his head again. He was inclined to take Len's appraisal with a pinch of salt. After all, who was Len? He was not some resident professor or local celebrity who could make a considered judgement.

Davies broke in. 'It's going to be pretty awkward for him now, isn't it? What I mean is,' he struggled to put into words what was in his mind, 'well, to put it bluntly, Len, no offence intended mind, but it's this. If he's not a nutter any more, how does he come off with his disability allowance and all that stuff? You say that he is very clever, and I believe you because I've talked to him, but he's thirty-two years old; never had a job in his life, got no qualifications and had no schooling. It's going to be an interesting couple of months for the lot of you, providing that is that he doesn't have a relapse.'

'Well, there is that about it,' said Len. 'But the way that he can do figures in his head, he would make a marvellous bookie. Maybe he could go self-employed, or something like that.' He drifted away and Reggie and Davies resumed their customary positions at the end of the bar.

'Something happened up at High Tor or somewhere around there,' said Davies. 'I'll bet that when the doctor examines him he'll find a big bump or something on his skull, you mark my words.' And he walked down the bar to serve a small group of regulars.

Reggie swilled his drink around in the glass, thinking. He often walked up to High Tor with Waldorf, though he hadn't been there lately. It was an odd place in itself. It was the same as a volcano, only in miniature. If you walked to the top and looked in you could see that it was concave in the middle. It had been explained away as a foible of the Ice Age, a crater formed when some huge boulders were swirled around. It was about a couple of hundred yards across and was covered in blackberry bushes and small scrubby trees. In the summer it was used by lovers, but on winter nights it was shunned by most people, except poachers after the rabbits of which there were thousands. A voice interrupted his thoughts. It was Daft Jim.

'Hello Mr Bagshott-Hawkes. How are you? Here, let me buy you a drink.'

Reggie was taken aback. The voice was almost cultured and being addressed in such a civilised manner, with an air of familiarity, left him stuck for words. He had hardly ever spoken to Jim, except to buy him the odd packet of crisps or nuts and raisins over the bar. He nodded, muttering a word of thanks, and put his empty glass on the counter, glancing at Davies who was casting a sardonic eye at him. He felt embarrassed.

'I. . . er . . . I don't know what to say . . . er . . . how are you?' The banality of his words hit him.

'Fine, thanks.' With a grin at Reggie's obvious discomfiture.

'I . . . don't know what to say. I'm . . . happy for you.'

'That's all right, Mr Bagshott-Hawkes. I know how you feel.'

'I . . . er . . . hear you're good at maths.'

'Yes, I am.' No false modesty there.

Reggie thought for a minute.

'What's the square root of three hundred and sixty-one?' he asked. He knew the answer because it had been in that morning's *Daily Mail* quiz.

'Nineteen', said Jim without a second's hesitation.

Reggie looked at him. He remembered what Len had said about Jim being able to read. He wondered if the family took the *Mail*. He didn't think so. The *Sun* or the *Mirror* more likely. He'd try him again. He racked his brains for a puzzle that he knew the answer to. He thought of the problems of the office.

'What would be the cost of an insurance policy if it was two hundred and thirty-two pounds less thirty per cent?'

'One hundred and sixty-two pounds forty.'

Reggie looked at him in amazement. He couldn't do that. There was only one member of his staff who could get anywhere near as good as that, Brenda Millsom, and that was because she ate, drank and slept insurance.

'How's Waldorf?' asked Jim, and they both turned and looked at Waldorf who was watching them from under half-closed eyes.

'Oh, he's all right,' said Reggie, 'aren't you, boy?' He was rewarded, much to his surprise, by a rumbling growl and the hackles on Waldorf's back stood up.

'Come on, boy,' said Reggie and moved towards

his dog. Waldorf skittered away under the chairs, knocking one or two of them over with a crash that caught everyone's attention. Jim said, 'I think it's me he's scared of.'

'Nonsense,' said Reggie, 'he's seen you hundreds of times. It must be something else. Come on, Waldorf. Don't play silly buggers, there's a good boy.' Waldorf scuttled to the door and gazed up at it then around at Reggie, whining. At that moment someone opened it from the other side and Waldorf was gone; out into the darkness like a bullet from a gun, knocking off his feet the chap who was walking in. Reggie and Jim rushed to help him to his feet but Jackie Hiscocks handed them off laughing, much to Reggie's relief. 'What's the matter with Waldorf tonight then? They've been telling those shaggy dog stories again to upset him, haven't they?' and he made his way to the bar laughing at his own joke.

'Here, let me buy you a drink,' said Reggie, walking up behind him, feeling uncomfortable. 'I must apologise for my dog. He's not usually like that . . .' He tailed off miserably.

'No thanks, I'm fine. Hadn't you better go and see where he's gone? He was in a bit of a hurry last time I saw him,' said Jackie, and turned back to the bar still laughing.

Reggie went to the door and looked out into the darkness. Waldorf had vanished. He returned to the bar and, apologising to Davies and Jim, quickly sank his gin and left. What could have got into the dog? Not like him at all.

He found Waldorf waiting for him around the corner at the end of the street. When the dog saw that Reggie was alone, he came up and wound himself around Reggie's legs for all the world like some monster cat. Reggie reached down and patted Waldorf and fondled his ears. He was unused to such expressions of affection. He was touched.

'Dammit, something must have upset the silly old sod,' he thought. He wondered what it could have been. They reached home without meeting anyone else on the way, Waldorf sticking so close to Reggie that a couple of times Reggie caught him with his heel.

'Definitely something wrong tonight. Haven't had to call him once all the way back from the pub,' he said to Lucy when he got in. 'That Daft Jim was in the pub, and you'll never guess. He's not daft any more. Always thought there was something not quite kosher about that family. Trying a new tack, if you ask me. He'll have to work for a living now like everyone else. Mind you, he did a couple of mental arithmetic things for me that bowled me over. I still can't figure out how he did it. Didn't get a real chance to talk to him because we had the shenanigans with him,' here nodding at Waldorf. He went on to relate the story of Daft Jim who wasn't daft any more, and after tea and more chat around the fire it was off to bed.

Chapter Three

Saturday morning, the tenth, dawned cold and bright. The sun was shining at an oblique angle through the windows that took up all of one wall of the large, airy dining room. 'October can throw up some nice days,' thought Reggie as he and Lucy ate their usual leisurely breakfast. The central heating made a small bubbling noise in the radiators and he made a mental note to bleed them as soon as he got the chance. He carried on with breakfast, reading the paper. Last night at the pub came back to him and he remarked on it to Lucy.

'Might pop in there again tonight,' he said, heaping marmalade on to his toast. 'See if that daft old bugger,' nodding in Waldorf's direction, 'acts up again.'

'Reggie,' exclaimed Lucy, 'your memory.' She clicked her tongue in exasperation. 'We've got George and Molly coming tonight. Now I did tell you, and I wish that you didn't swear so.'

Reggie looked suitably chastised. Wiping his lips with his serviette he nodded.

'Yes, yes, I remember, Lucy. It just slipped my

memory, that's all. George and Molly. Nice old pair. Always at home with them.' Lucy nodded and started to clear away the breakfast things.

'Now come on, Reggie, we're meeting the Barlows at the Angel at twelve-thirty, and I have to get quite a lot done in town before then. I have to get some odds and ends for the basket class and do some of my own shopping, so you'll have to get a move on.'

Reggie finished his coffee and dutifully helped clear the table and load the dishwasher.

The day passed pleasantly enough and, after lunch in the Angel, Reggie was comfortably drowsy when they arrived home at around four-thirty. He roused himself with an effort and spent half an hour or so bleeding the central heating then, putting on his old overcoat and battered trilby and changing his shoes for his walking boots, he picked up his stout knobbly walking stick and Waldorf's lead and headed towards the back door. 'Going out with Waldorf to blow the cobwebs away,' he called up the stairs to Lucy who was in the spare bedroom sorting out supplies for one of her latest WI projects.

'All right dear, don't be long will you, they'll be here at eight.'

'No, won't be long,' he shouted up the stairs and walked out of the back door accompanied by Waldorf, who had suddenly appeared as if by magic on hearing the lead and walking stick being taken out of the cupboard.

The sun was sinking in the west behind the far-away mountain range and there was a pronounced nip in the air as they walked up the lane towards High Tor. Reggie hadn't been up there for some time and it was only the interest generated in the pub last night that had decided him on it now. His mind went back to the previous day as he strode along. What a day!

He had arrived at the office at eight o'clock, near enough. The staff had arrived punctually at nine and there had been a chorus of 'Happy Birthdays' to Samantha Smith followed by present giving. She was a popular girl with a strong, outgoing personality and was never at a loss for a quick answer. Reggie had been standing in the doorway at the back of the main office as the staff came in and the news of Samantha's birthday took him by surprise – not that he would have bought her a card or been asked to contribute to a present, but he would now have to react to the news of the birthday and he didn't quite know how to.

As he watched the girl receiving her presents and birthday cards, bestowing kisses on the cheeks of her colleagues as she received them, he had felt called upon to say something.

'Er, er, happy birthday, Miss Smith,' he said awkwardly as she pushed past him on the way down to the cloakroom.

'Oh. Thank you, boss,' she said with delight, putting her free hand around him and planting a kiss on his cheek before scampering off with a twinkle in her eyes.

He felt himself going red with embarrassment and could see the rest of the staff watching him with barely concealed amusement. He turned quickly back into his room and, shutting the door, went straight back to his desk and tried to concentrate on the paperwork in front of him, cursing himself for feeling the way that he did.

It had been afternoon before Reggie came out to see if everything was going smoothly but, like all good offices, the place virtually ran itself. He saw that the cork notice and memorandum board on the wall behind the counter had a dozen or more birthday cards pinned on it. He wondered who they were all from and stopped to have a look. Apart from the staff, the rest were from customers and agents, and the sexual overtones of most of them made him blush. Just thinking back on it now made him feel uncomfortable. What had happened to the balloons and bottles of champers and cuddly teddies that had been depicted on cards in his youth?

Evening mist rose out of the ditch at the side of the road as they walked along. They reached the gate that led to the top of High Tor as the sun was about to meet the horizon. Waldorf hung back and sat down about twenty yards behind Reggie.

'Come on, Waldorf, not another bout of bloody histrionics,' shouted Reggie, puzzled by the dog's behaviour. Normally he was over the gate and on up to the rim hunting for rabbits as soon as they arrived. He returned to Waldorf and as he approached the dog started to walk back the way they had come, obviously eager to get away from the place. But Reggie had other ideas. Grasping Waldorf's collar, he clipped on the lead and started walking up the hill again.

'Come on, Waldorf.' Tug, tug. 'Now come on.' He heaved on the lead until he realised that he was almost strangling the dog, but still Waldorf wouldn't budge, so, after much pulling and shouting and threatening, Reggie gave up and tied the lead to one of the bushes growing at the side of the road. Still panting and puffing from his exertions, he made his way up to the rim, making promises to himself to get fit and lose more of his fat. Reaching the rim, he stood and looked into the crater.

What was it about this place that was putting such fear into Waldorf, he wondered. In the fading light, the bushes tended to look like one dark mass. As his eyes grew more accustomed to the poor visibility, it seemed to him that the bushes were flattened in the centre of the crater, in a circle about fifty yards across. He squinted to get a better sight, turning his head slightly to the right to favour his left, best eye, and stopped, frozen with surprise. He turned his head a fraction and the image vanished and all he could see were the flattened bushes. He turned his head slightly to the right again and there it was. It was like looking through a sliver of glass that gave a different slant on what was really there. What he could see now, the thing that was flattening the bushes, sent a shiver quirking up his spine. A SPACE SHIP!

'Don't be ridiculous,' he said to himself. He felt panic starting to rise in him and looked around. Nobody about; he hadn't expected there to be. He turned his head again to find the window in space and yes, there it was. *A space ship.* He had to keep his head perfectly still. A small movement to the right or left caused the picture to vanish. In the glow coming from the machine he could see small beings moving about, and other objects of a much more defined shape. He thought they must be vehicles of some kind although they did not seem to have any wheels. They hung over the ground, much like a hovercraft, but without the noise. He wondered if he ought to hide. Perhaps they could see him. Panic hit him and his lower stomach twittered and gurgled. He had to get back to the village fast and bring somebody up here to see this. Somebody in authority. But the trouble was that as soon as he made any movement, the scene disappeared again.

He would have to make some mark so that when he brought people back he would have no trouble finding the exact spot. But how? He searched his pockets and found his penknife. With shaking hands he opened it and, squatting down, diligently cut a groove around each foot as fast as he could, throwing the strips of turf away into the bushes. Each foot now stood on a small island, and he straightened up, putting his knife back in his pocket, and checked for his small peephole in space.

He found it – and to his horror saw that he was surrounded by the silvery beings. They were about half his size, with big heads in comparison to their bodies, and large oriental eyes that seemed to be all of one colour, without a pupil. They had one of the peculiar vehicles with them. One of the spacemen was pointing something like a gun at him. He turned to run and the nightmare vanished only to be replaced by another. He couldn't move his legs. He struggled with all his might to get his limbs working, but paralysis was creeping up his body. He heard himself screaming, 'Help! Help!' as a terrible fear overcame his self control. A banshee howling and growling broke into his consciousness. It was Waldorf. An irrational thought leapt into his head: 'I hope somebody finds him or he'll starve to death.' It was almost his last conscious thought. He felt himself being lifted from the ground and plonked down into the space buggy. Then darkness overtook him.

Chapter Four

Lucy stood at the front door rubbing her hands. Where was Reggie? He was not often late and even if he was, it was only minutes, not an hour or more. The Turpins would be here at eight, and it was gone quarter to now. Surely he hadn't gone to the pub tonight after all and forgotten about them. She switched the outside light on so that George and Molly could see to get out of their car safely then went back in and reached for the telephone.

'No,' said Mrs Davies, 'I haven't seen him tonight, but he doesn't usually come in on a Saturday in any case. Hang on. I'll go and ask in the bar. Someone may have seen him.' She was back in a moment. 'No,' she said, 'he's not been in. Like I said, it's too crowded for him on a Saturday. If he shows up I'll tell him that you want him and to get on home. Bye bye, got to fly, we're up to our eyes,' and she rang off.

Lucy slowly put the phone down. The sound of a car outside sent her hurrying to the front door and she stood there waiting as the Turpins walked up the path. 'Come in,' she said, 'and I'll get you a drink. I'm sorry that Reggie isn't here, but he took Waldorf for a walk to blow away the cobwebs, and hasn't got back yet.' She leaned over to Molly and put her cheek to hers for a perfunctory kiss.

'How long's he been gone?' asked George.

'He left sometime between five or six,' said Lucy, looking at the clock in the hallway.

'Perhaps he's down the pub?' said George.

'No,' said Lucy. 'I've phoned the pub and they haven't seen him.'

'Phone the police. Get hold of Gus Mcleod, he never goes out till late on a Saturday when the pub shuts and then has a sly pint with Davies in the back room.'

'Do you think I ought to?' said Lucy. 'Perhaps he's stopped talking somewhere.'

George snorted. 'Not Reggie. He knew we were coming tonight and it's not in character for the man not to be here to meet his guests. Phone Gus up, or phone the hospital, but I would phone Gus. If there's been an accident, he would be the first to know.'

The local police station was in a building that doubled as a normal house. Gus Mcleod worked when it suited him or the job. Crime, as it was in the cities and towns, didn't exist on his beat. He had a car and a bicycle, and except when the weather was bad, or he was in a hurry, it was the bike that he used. He found that when riding the bike he could see much more of what was going on. Gus was drinking a mug of tea, his tenth that day, when the phone rang. Unhurriedly he picked it up. 'Police,' he said and listened to what was being said.

'No sign at all?' he asked neutrally. He had long ago learned to be low key when dealing with a fraught situation. Daft Jim flitted through his mind; that was about a week ago. High Tor, wasn't it, he'd searched for Jim?

'I'll get the car out, Mrs Bagshott-Hawkes,' he said. 'Have a drive around and see if I can spot him.' Putting the phone down, he reached for his mug of tea and finished it off. He thought about Mr Bagshott-Hawkes. An ordinary chap. Never any bother. If they were all like him, there'd be no need for a police force. Getting to his feet with a sigh he called to Jane, his wife. 'Got to go out, love. Don't know how long I am going to be. Bagshott-Hawkes has vanished. At least, he hasn't come home from his walk yet. Silly old bugger might have fallen down a ditch or something; still, the bloody dog should have come home at least. I'll try not to be too long.' And with that he shut the door and was gone

First he drove to Reggie's house. After all, he might have turned up since Mrs Bagshott-Hawkes phoned. He parked behind the Turpins' car on the drive. The front door of the house was already open and Lucy was standing there with George and Molly behind her.

'No sign of him then,' said Gus. It was more of a statement than a question. 'No idea where he went?

There's only two ways that he can go. Up the lane towards High Tor, or down into the village past the pub. If he went past the pub at this time of night – what time did he go out? About five? Half past?'

'Somewhere around there,' said Lucy. 'I'm not too certain.'

'Damn. Too early,' said Gus. 'Still, they may have seen him in the shop, that might still have been open. I'll pop down there and see if anyone saw him and I'll go into the pub and ask as well. Was he normal? Not acting funny? Sorry, but I've got to ask, was he OK?'

Lucy nodded.

'No sign of the dog? Now don't get alarmed, but sometimes, if there has been an accident – and I'm not saying there has – but if there has been, it's usual for the dog to come home all agitated.'

'Not with Waldorf,' Lucy asserted heatedly. 'He would stay with Reggie if anything had happened. That dog would lay down his life for either of us.' She started to cry. Molly leaped up and put her arms around her.

'Come on, Lucy,' she said. 'Don't think the worst, there's probably some simple explanation. He's probably fallen down and sprained his ankle or something and Waldorf is staying with him "on guard", as it were. You'll see. It'll be all right. Come on, let's see if there's any tea left in the pot, or if not I'll make you a fresh one.' She dragged Lucy off to the kitchen.

Gus looked at George. 'Well, sir, I think I'd better

make a start. You'll be here for a bit, I take it? I'll have a scout round and get back to you. If we don't find him it's going to be a long night.' He went out to his car and was gone.

His first call was to the shop. No, they hadn't seen him or the dog. They'd shut at six as usual. It had been a bit quiet, quieter than normal as a matter of fact, and they would have noticed Reggie and Waldorf if they had gone by.

He thanked them and went on down to the pub. It was packed and he went into the bar first, nodding at Davies who looked at him quizzically. He quickly told the landlord what had happened and asked if he could question everybody in there as to whether they had seen Reggie. Davies nodded. Picking up a heavy ashtray, Gus banged on the bar, calling for quiet, and asked his question. No one had seen Reggie. Davies accompanied Gus to the entrance hall of the pub and asked him what was going on.

'I don't know,' said Gus. 'I don't like it at all, to tell you the truth. It's too much like last week when young Contrell went missing. Never did find out what happened to him. He said that he remembered walking out of the gate up at High Tor, so I'm going off in the car to have a look up there first – or last, come to that, 'cause if he isn't up there, I don't know where to look. I'll pop in as usual later on, that is if I find him safe and sound.' And he gave a wave and went back to his car. He drove out of the pub car park and turned back up the road past Reggie's towards High Tor, arriving at the gate leading up to the summit where he was surprised to see a figure that he knew at once wasn't Reggie. He pulled in and stopped the car. Daft Jim turned and watched him.

'Hello, Mr Mcleod,' he said. 'Are you looking for Mr Bagshott-Hawkes? Well he isn't here, or Waldorf. I've looked all over the crater and around it and there's no sign of them, and really, if they were here, Waldorf would have let me know because he's gone right off me and he barks and makes a fuss when I go near him.'

Gus looked at him. He still couldn't get used to the fact that the man was normal.

'What are you doing up here, Jim, anyway?' he asked quietly.

'Well, I was in the pub when Mrs Bagshott-Hawkes phoned and I was thinking that it was a bit odd, her phoning. Mr Bagshott-Hawkes isn't like that. Regimented, that's him. It was up here that something happened to me so I thought that I'd come up and have a look around. It's a funny thing, them both vanishing just the same way that I did. Never did find out what happened to me. I've thought and thought about it, but my mind is a complete blank from the time that I left the house until I came to, walking down towards this gate. I must have come from somewhere up there to be going through the gate the way I was. But they're definitely not up there.'

Gus walked through the gate followed by Jim and together they climbed to the top of the crater. The wind soughing through the trees sounded eerie but any shouting or barking could have been heard quite easily. Gus shouted, 'Mr Hawkes! Mr Bagshott-Hawkes!' Nothing. Another shout. Again nothing. They walked around the rim of the crater with Gus shining his torch around and about until they arrived back at the spot where they had started. They had heard a couple of rabbits start up and scoot off and, as Gus said, if there had been anybody there, the rabbits would have been long gone.

They went back to the car and Gus told Jim to get in. He turned the car around and they drove back to Reggie's house. All the lights were on and the front door was wide open so Gus got out of the car and went straight in. He stood just inside the entrance hall and looked about. There were now about a dozen people in the house and the buzz of conversation stopped as he walked in, all heads swivelling round to look at him.

'No sign of them at all, then?' asked George Turpin, and gesturing to the others in the room he went on, 'These people came up from the pub to see if they could help but we said to wait until you came back in case you'd found them.'

Gus shook his head. 'Not a sign of them anywhere. I've got Jim Contrell outside in the car. He went up on his own to High Tor when he heard about it and that's where I found him. That's where he came to, if you remember, when he vanished last week, and he thought that there might be a connection. But there was no sign of them at all. It's no good us going out tonight with a search party, as we don't know where to begin, so I suggest that someone stays here with Mrs Bagshott-Hawkes and we make an early start. If we all meet here at about seven in the morning then by the time we get up to High Tor it will be daylight.' There was some murmuring of dissent from the people sitting in the lounge.

'Now listen,' said Gus, 'use your common sense. I understand how you feel, but think. What can we do out there that we haven't done already? Not a lot. And we may destroy footprints that could lead us to them if we go traipsing about up there in the dark. No. That's it. We'll meet here at seven o'clock in the morning and do a proper search. Bring some ordnance maps and binoculars and some hot soup in thermos flasks because if we find them, they'll be famished. See you all in the morning. Good night.' He walked to the door but as he reached it he turned back and said, 'If he does come in, phone me at the station and let me know. Good night again.'

When he got back into the car Jim was filled with curiosity.

'What happened?' he asked.

'Not a lot,' said Gus. 'I told them that it was no good going up there or anywhere else until we had some daylight, but they didn't like it. Couple of them were all for going out searching now, but I think I scotched that idea. I can understand how they feel, but I honestly don't think we could do any good by going out tonight.' He put the car in gear and backed out of the drive.

'Where are you going now?' he asked Jim as he was driving out.

'Back to the pub,' said Jim. 'Perhaps some of the late arrivals might have seen him.'

'I doubt it,' said Gus. 'Davies would have phoned and let us know. I think I'll pop in as well. Show my face. Let them see that the law's still busy even at this time on a Saturday night.' He grinned in the dark, his white teeth flashing as he looked around at Jim. 'I'll have a word with Davies, and then I'll go home and have an early night and see you in the morning.'

They drove a couple of hundred yards down the road to the pub, parked and went in to the bar, where they immediately became the centre of attraction in the main topic of conversation.

Chapter Five

On Sunday morning, Reggie awoke with a start. The sun was warm on his back and he lay there for a second or two trying to figure out where he was and how in the devil he had got there. He appeared to be lying on his stomach on the grass. He raised his head and looked around.

There was a body lying on the grass beside him, wearing an old overcoat like his. He tried to stand up to go over and look at it, but found that his legs wouldn't behave themselves no matter how hard he tried. There was something stuck on his face that was blocking his vision, a grey hairy object that appeared to be attached to his nose. He put up a hand to pull it off, and into his vision came a grey hairy leg with a paw on the end which tapped the grey hairy thing on his face, and it hurt. He looked down at himself, his stomach heaving. A dog's body. He looked over his shoulder at his back and rolled over the ground with shock. He was a dog. He raised his arms and examined them. Dog's legs, and what was that scar on the left one? He recognised it: Waldorf! It couldn't be. He was never inside Waldorf's body?

He gave a loud cry of panic and fear and heard a terrible noise issuing from his throat. A memory from last night came flooding back. Waldorf howling. He realised, now, that it was he himself who was making the noise.

He closed his eyes. A nightmare. Please God, a nightmare, please, please, let it be that. His heart thudded and the sun was still warm on his back and the smell of grass was in his nostrils. He opened his eyes again and the scene was unchanged. He tried to stagger to his feet but found that he couldn't; that is, he couldn't stand on his feet like a human.

He dropped back on to all fours, looking around for some explanation of what had happened to him, and again saw the body lying beside him in his old overcoat. A battered trilby was lying some distance from its head which now had its eyes open and was watching him. Reggie stared back in disbelief. It was him. He walked on all fours, which he found he could do if he didn't stop to think about it, over to the body which suddenly sat up and eyed him warily. He tried to talk, to ask this figure what was going on, but all that came out was a series of whines and guttural noises that seemed to alarm his old body and made it back away in fright.

A noise issued from the body's lips, three short, sharp noises accompanied by a facial expression that reminded Reggie instantly of Waldorf. He collapsed back on to his haunches, helpless terror beginning to take over.

He was in Waldorf's body, and Waldorf was in his.

He started to run around in a panic and fell over a couple of times as he tried consciously to control the four legs, but he quickly found that if he left them to their own devices they adjusted themselves. Soon panic had taken a grip on him and he was hurtling around making a dreadful howling noise, crashing through the blackberry bushes and brambles in a way that would have scared the hell out of the rabbit population, if there had been any about.

'It's them.' The thought shrieked through his head. 'Those sodding things. Those blobs I saw before . . . before what? The bastards, they've done this to me.'

The footprints. Where were the footprints? He staggered to his hind legs and tried to look around but he couldn't keep still long enough to see exactly where he was. He gave a dreadful howl that would have frightened a werewolf. The noise frightened him even more as he ran up and down searching for the footprints, becoming increasingly panic-stricken when he couldn't find them.

Waldorf, for it was indeed he, in Reggie's body, decided to join in the fun and the next thing Reggie knew was that a big fat man with a ridiculous little moustache and lank strips of hair sticking out of the sides of an otherwise bald head was gambolling through the brambles with him on his hands and knees but, without the protection of hair around his face and hands, was soon bleeding from a multitude of scratches.

The sight brought Reggie to a halt. The overcoat was already in shreds; the buttons gone, as were his shoes and one of his socks.

Waldorf, in Reggie's body, finally came to a stop, his breath coming in terrible rasps, and he sank down on to the grass in a small clearing.

Reggie went up to him but Waldorf was too far gone to do anything except wave a futile hand in Reggie's general direction. Perspiration ran down his face in a way that it never had in Reggie's occupation of the body.

Heart attack, that was it, Reggie thought in panic. The way Waldorf had pushed his, Reggie's, old body around for the last five minutes was enough to kill it. He'd have to get help. He turned and ran out of the crater and around the rim until he recognised where he was, then down the hill on the other side and on, as fast as his legs would carry him into the lane, where he saw a group of people who were obviously out searching for something or somebody. Of course. Him and Waldorf!

Gus, the local policeman, was talking to Lucy and had a couple of sheets of paper in his hand. Reggie broke into a fast gallop and heard a cry go up, 'Here's Waldorf,' and all heads turned. Lucy ran towards him and he sprang at her, knocking her over in his enthusiasm.

'Waldorf, Waldorf! Where is he, where's Reggie? Is he all right?' She hugged him and Reggie was standing over her and trying to pull her up but he couldn't do it and he was moaning and groaning and howling all at the same time, trying to scream, 'Lucy, Lucy, it's me, me, *me*.' The crowd moved in to drag Lucy back to her feet and he was up on his hind legs trying to hug her and tell her that *he* was Reggie and that Waldorf was up there, waving a paw, when he suddenly realised that he was naked! He fell to the ground and rolled up in a ball, trying to hide his penis from the world with his two front paws, but still screaming and howling, going what appeared to the crowd to be barking mad.

Lucy broke away from the people who were trying to brush the leaves and dust off her clothes from where she had been knocked on the road and reached over, hugging the grey old dog to her. Still hiding his penis as best he could, he sobbed to her that he was Reggie but all that came out was the sound of a dog in terrible pain. Gus and some of the rest of the search party leaned over and stroked him.

'He looks hurt to me,' said Gus. 'Come on, boy. Let's have a look at you.'

Reggie howled. It was the last thing that he wanted. Gus ran his hand down Reggie's stomach and tried to loosen the paws pressed tightly to his penis.

'Come on, boy. Let's see what you've got down there.' He jumped back as Reggie gave a snarl in the best Waldorf manner then lurched to his feet, still holding one paw between his legs, and staggered off up the road as fast as he could on three legs.

He had put about fifty yards between himself and the crowd when he stopped and looked around. That was OK. They couldn't see anything now. He gave a howl and started to walk back up to High Tor, looking over his shoulder to see if they were following. They were.

He would show them what was what. He would take them and show them Waldorf in *his*, Reggie's, body and they would see. A little doubt flickered across his mind and he brushed it away. *Of course* they would see. So he started to walk faster and they got the message and quickened their pace.

'I hope he's leading us back to where Reggie is,' said Gus, looking hopefully at Reggie, who was now about a hundred yards ahead of them, howling and coughing and bouncing up and down on his hind legs trying to make them go faster. 'If ever a dog was trying to tell us something . . .' He sagely nodded his head.

'Go on, boy, show us where your master is,' he shouted at Reggie.

Reggie, hearing this, gave another howl and loped off even faster.

'Show you where my master is indeed,' his mind screamed, and the frustration was reflected in the ferocious snarls issuing from his muzzle which was now dripping with foamy saliva. 'I *am* the master, you bloody dimwit. Stupid damn fool . . . Should be out there looking for those bloody spacemen or whatever they are. If you'd done your job properly in the first place, we'd not be in this bloody state now.'

He stopped and glared back at them, trying to make his temper come off the boil. He'd never had a temper in his normal life. Old Mr Cool, they'd called him. Well, they should see him now. He thought sourly that it would be better if he humoured them until they saw Waldorf and then they would know that there had been some horrible mistake and would all do their best to put things right, so he started back up the road. He might as well go along with it until he could put the record straight.

Looking behind him again he saw that he was travelling much too fast for the posse so he sat down and howled for a few moments then got to his feet and started to head off towards High Tor again. He thought for a moment about treating them like sheep and running behind them snapping at their heels, but better sense prevailed and he decided to run on ahead and make them chase after him. Gus was in his police car at the back of the posse with Lucy in the passenger seat and as Reggie glanced back again he saw the car edge past the crowd, closely followed by the gentlemen of the press in another car (where on earth had they come from?) and begin to catch him up. He set off again at a much faster pace, and in a short while he was back at the spot where he had left Waldorf.

BUT WALDORF WAS GONE!

Reggie turned back to face the searchers now arriving in dribs and drabs at the clearing, having parked their cars on the edge of the lane. He wasn't too worried now about being naked as the ferns and bracken shielded most of him from their gaze. Howling, and still making awful noises, he turned and, raising his right front leg, pointed to the spot in the clearing where he had left Waldorf. He tried at the same time to say, 'Well, this is where I left him,' but all that came out was a series of whines and howls.

Gus moved up to him and, leaning down, took hold of his paw and turned it over to look at the pad.

'There, there, old boy, hold still. What's the matter with this paw? You got a thorn in it or something?'

Reggie tugged his paw away and, snapping angrily at Gus, turned and ran on into the bushes. He soon came to his overcoat which was in a worse mess than when he had last seen it. He gave a howl and stood on his back legs so that the searchers could see him over the tops of the bramble bushes, and soon, with much beating of sticks, they joined him. The overcoat was discovered and handed to Lucy who gave a little cry of recognition and identified it as Reggie's; and was captured by the cameraman with tears streaming down her face.

Reggie, back on all fours and peering, with his head down, along the narrow trail that wandered through the bushes and brambles, saw up ahead of him another garment: his jacket. Then his trousers. And so on until his whole wardrobe had been found. Reggie sat down on his haunches – then he spotted his blood-stained underpants. His body was going to be completely starkers when they found it.

Little shivers ran up and down his spine at the thought and for a moment he contemplated giving up the search, or leading the posse off on a false trail. What else could he do? There was no way he was going to let them see his body in the nude, even if he wasn't in occupation at the time.

He was worrying needlessly. He heard Gus and Lucy calling him, 'Waldorf, Waldorf,' and there was a crashing in the bushes from up ahead and to his left. A shout went up, 'There's Reggie!', followed by cries of disbelief and horror and a scream from Lucy as the bloody, naked figure of her husband emerged from the brambles. He jumped on her and knocked her flat on her back, licking her face, uttering moans and groans and shrieks, all of it being recorded by the newsmen.

That Lucy didn't recognise her husband and thought that she was going to be raped by this wild man of the woods went without saying. She had, as you will recall, never seen Reggie naked. And she had certainly never seen him in the buff covered with blood with his hair sticking out and a wild look in his eyes.

The intensity of her screams terrified everyone around her and Reggie (in Waldorf's body) was no exception. The hair all along his back stood up and, naked or not, when he recovered from the shattering effect of the noise he rushed forward before any of the men could move and sank his teeth firmly into Waldorf's backside, trying to drag him off.

It was so unexpected that Lucy, flat on her back with Waldorf on top of her, had the breath knocked out of her, and it was a few seconds before Gus was able to marshal his boggled senses and call for help to drag Waldorf and Reggie off.

Waldorf thought that Gus was going to join Reggie in what he assumed would be an attack on Lucy and he turned on him in a rage, snapping and snarling, with his blood-smeared face so contorted and so madly fearsome that Gus fell back in fright. When he had gathered his wits, he called for help again and he and his men moved in on Waldorf and Reggie, attempting to separate them. Reggie, seeing reinforcements arrive, let go of Waldorf's buttock and sat back down in the ferns.

He looked at the terrible bite marks on Waldorf's backside and the thought struck him that he must be the only man in the world who had inflicted a bite on his own behind.

A crazed Waldorf in Reggie's seventeen-stone body

brushed off the men like flies and the small clearing was beginning to look like a battlefield. Bodies were lying on the ground. Gus was bitten and so were a few helpers, until Reggie's old body could no longer keep up with the demands of Waldorf's brain, and collapsed. Gus took out his handcuffs and in no time at all Waldorf's arms were pinioned behind his back. One of the men took off his leather belt and they were able to secure his legs as well.

Waldorf could offer no more resistance so they turned him on to his stomach to hide his nakedness from the women and one of the heavier men sat on his buttocks, after putting a fairly clean handkerchief over the bite marks. Gus meanwhile went back to his car and radioed back to base for an ambulance and a doctor as quickly as possible. Lucy cradled Waldorf's head in her lap and used her handkerchief to clean away some of the blood. The newsmen were beside themselves. What a break. What a story!

Waldorf was quite content to lie there getting his breath back and being fussed over by Lucy. After all, she was the only one who ever fussed over him at home, so there was nothing unusual in that, and besides, he was too whacked to do anything else.

Lucy looked around helplessly as one of the men came over to throw a coat over her husband's naked body. Reggie was trying to lick her as she cleaned him up and she moved her hand away and patted him on the head, while tears flowed down her cheeks.

And all the time Reggie, in Waldorf's body, sat in the ferns and watched with his mind in a turmoil. What could he do?

'I should be jumping up and down and howling and telling them that there has been some terrible mistake and that *I* am Reggie,' he thought. 'But if I did start jumping up and down, there's no way that I would be brought a nice friendly doctor with a bedside manner. Oh no, they'd bring in the vet and I'd be put down as quick as a flash, and they'd say rabies or something equally foul to justify what they'd done.' He lay down and waited for Gus to return from his car. 'Shouldn't be too long now, Mrs Bagshott-Hawkes,' he said when he came back. 'They got on to your own doctor and he'll be right up.'

The little group of people that had gathered were now chatting amongst themselves. Some were smoking and one rather unkempt looking man with a couple of days' growth of grey beard had produced a hip flask and was offering it around.

Reggie looked at his old self with horror. That was him. That was his fat, sweaty body they were all staring at. If he ever regained possession, that stupid moustache would come off, and about three stone of ugly fat. And that hair! He shook his head in disgust.

The arrival of the doctor was closely followed by an ambulance with a crew of two. Then came a small police van with wire mesh over the windows. The drivers and passengers left their vehicles at the bottom of the hill and walked up, the crowd falling back to allow them through. The doctor, Dulcie Nicholas's husband, was an old friend of the Bagshott-Hawkes.

'Hello, Lucy,' he said. 'I see they found them, then.' Lucy turned to him with a sob.

'Oh, John,' she said, 'look at the state he's in. He's been like this since we found him, can't get a sensible word out of him. Always so particular about his appearance. Look at him now.' And the tears flowed faster.

John Nicholas handed Lucy over to Gus, saying that when he had seen to Reggie he would take her home and put her to bed with a sedative, and not to worry about Reggie. Maybe he had lost his memory, but he would be bound to make a full recovery in a couple of days once they got him to hospital and found out what had happened. Flanked by the two ambulance men, he made a cursory examination before they loaded Reggie (Waldorf) on to a stretcher.

Waldorf had feebly renewed his efforts to get friendly, this time with the doctor, whom he recognised as someone who used to bring him titbits. Waldorf looked a pitiable mess. By now, in Reggie's naked body, without the thick grey hair he was used to, he was chilled to the bone and was shivering to such an extent that the six men (Reggie's body proved too heavy for two men) had a job to carry him the short distance to the ambulance.

Reggie in Waldorf's body attempted to follow, but

they wouldn't allow him into the ambulance. 'We can't let a dog in here. It's not hygienic,' they said, and he started to create again. The burly policeman who had arrived with the police van produced a muzzle and dog's lead from a small bag that he was carrying and expertly grabbed Reggie. With Gus's help he deftly put the muzzle and lead on him and dragged him, screaming and snarling, to the police van. Opening the door, he roughly lifted him in and slammed the door shut behind him.

They drove off, following the ambulance, and stopped at Reggie's house while the ambulance continued to the hospital. They took Reggie around the back and clipped him up to the chain beside the garage by his slip collar, leaving him with a pat on the head, and a, 'There's a good old boy.'

He waited till they had all gone and, slipping his paw up under the slip chain, he pulled it up over his head and trotted off to the house. He needed to relieve himself and could not bring himself to be completely dog-like in that respect.

The house was locked but he knew where the back door key was hidden. He found it and, gripping the large old-fashioned key between his teeth, he managed to get it into the lock and turn it. Taking the key back out he put it back in its hiding place, and went into the house.

Five minutes later he was back in the yard. It was all very well needing to go to the toilet and wanting to use the facilities that he was used to but – and a very big but it was – human toilets were simply not designed for dogs. But he had to go so, with great mortification, he used the drain in the yard. When he had finished he dragged the hose over and, using his teeth again, turned on the tap and washed the evidence away.

Seven-year-old Jason in his tree house next door watched the proceedings with interest. When they were over he scrambled down and ran into his house full of excitement to tell his mum what he'd seen. He was received with the grown-up condescension that all kids of his age have to put up with.

'Oh, yes,' said his mum, 'and then I suppose he cleaned the windows and hung out the washing for good measure?' She shook her head in amusement. 'Kids! Let their imagination run away with them. Go on, Jason, get back out there, he's probably tuning up the car now, and you'll be missing it.'

Reggie, meanwhile, had gone back into the house to think. He was slumped in his, Reggie's, favourite armchair, his brain fairly steaming with the wild thoughts chasing each other frantically around his head.

'How can I tell people that I am Reggie?' was uppermost in his thoughts.

'I can't,' came back the obvious answer.

'Perhaps if I can write?' With that thought he was out of the chair and into the study, looking for some paper and a pencil or a ballpoint. He found all three. He tried to manoeuvre the paper on to the large blotter on the desk but found that that was beyond his capabilities, so he decided to write on the blotter if he could. He took the ballpoint in his mouth and tried to write 'Reggie' but the pen kept waggling in his teeth and all he achieved were crooked lines, saliva over the paper and dog hairs on the seat. He climbed down off the big leather executive chair in which he had sat so many times before whilst studying his war books and wandered disconsolately back into the lounge and his armchair. He glanced at the dog basket in the conservatory with disgust as he went by and made a mental note that if ever he regained his rightful place, that basket was going and Waldorf could have the use of this armchair for the rest of his life.

He was still lying there when he heard voices at the front door and Lucy came in with the doctor. He staggered off the chair and went to meet them, forgetting in his pleasure that he shouldn't be there at all, but in the yard, tied up. Lucy saw him coming towards her.

'Hello, Waldorf, how did you get in? We must have left the back door unlocked in all the excitement.' She patted his head and bent down to give him a hug. 'You looked after him, didn't you, Waldorf? Good old boy.' And tears started again. Reggie gave a moan of frustrated anguish at not being able to comfort her. The doctor looked at them and said in a kindly voice, 'Come on, Lucy, this isn't like you. Now, who can you get to stay with you for the rest of today and tonight? I'll send Dulcie over, I think. She'll look after you. Now don't say "no", that's a doctor's order, so go on upstairs and get into bed and I'll be up in a minute to give you a sedative. I'll just give Dulcie a quick ring.'

Reggie followed Lucy to the foot of the stairs. She turned. 'Now go back, Waldorf,' she said. 'You know you aren't allowed up here. There's a good boy.' She turned and carried on up the stairs. Reggie went back to his armchair and curled up in it, listening to the doctor talking to his wife.

'Yes, love, you'll be staying the night. I'm going to give her a fairly strong sleeping draught. Reggie? Oh, he seems to have gone completely off his chump. Poor devil. He's under sedation now and he'll be out till the morning, I should think. Then they'll have to start doing tests. It's not my province so I don't know much about that side of medicine and, quite frankly, I wouldn't know where to start in his case. See you later, love.'

Reggie gave up listening and thought again about his and Waldorf's predicament. Why had 'they' done this to them? Was it some kind of sick joke? Perhaps they were being studied as an experiment? He looked around to see if he was being observed by anything and remembered the peephole in space that he had stumbled on. Perhaps 'they' had one in this room and were looking through it right now. Perhaps they had seen him trying to use the toilet and had split their sides with amusement. He hoped that if they had, they had bloody well ruptured themselves.

The doorbell rang and the doctor came down to answer it but it was only Dulcie with an overnight bag, a little breathless from hurrying. After a short conversation they both went upstairs. Reggie lumbered off the chair and padded over to the bottom of the stairs. He could hear Lucy talking about him to Dulcie and could hear the break in her voice.

'Yes, they're doing tests in the morning, Dulcie. They have to wait until the sedative has worn off and cleared his system. They thought that he'd had a knock on the head but they can't find any mark or bruising. They've put him to bed and strapped him in just in case he wakes up violent. It's not like Reggie at all.' Here her voice broke altogether and Reggie loped away so as not to hear the muffled sobs. If only there was something he could do. He felt an irrational surge of anger towards Waldorf, just lying there in hospital, not making any effort to clear up this mess.

He recognised the futility of the thought almost as soon as it came, and he visualised Waldorf in the morning all wired up as specialists and psychologists surrounded his bed and tried to unscramble his brain.

'Fat chance,' Reggie thought unkindly. 'Waldorf doesn't have a brain to unscramble. Now if someone were to shout "DINNER" at him, the little trembling pens would probably fly off the graph paper.' The thought of dinner brought home to him the fact that he hadn't eaten – since yesterday lunchtime in the pub. Gosh! That seemed ages away now. He trotted out to the kitchen and, gripping the refrigerator door handle with his teeth, pulled the door open. There was half of a tinned ham on a plate, covered in cling wrap, some cheese, also covered in film, and milk, eggs, a carton of clotted cream, and trifle and custard, obviously ready for last night's visitors, who must have gone home hungry. Hearing footsteps on the stairs, he shut the fridge door and was back lying in his chair when Dulcie and the doctor came in. A quick peck on Dulcie's cheek and the doctor was gone, saying something about having to get back to the surgery as he was on stand-by. Dulcie busied herself in the kitchen, filling a tray with tea and biscuits which she carried off upstairs to Lucy.

She hadn't got half way up the stairs before Reggie was back in the fridge. Gripping the plate with the ham on it between his teeth, he put it carefully on the floor and shut the fridge door. Getting the cling film off was more difficult than he had thought. Finally he held the plate between his paws and pulled the film off with his teeth, then carried it over to the pedal bin and dropped it in.

He made short work of the ham after he discovered that his dental set-up didn't lend itself to masticating his food. Wolfing it down was the order of the day. He suddenly realised why Waldorf was so quick at clearing his plate. No leisurely enjoyment of food for him. He found the large tongue useful for clearing every last scrap, and then, with a sigh of regret that it was all gone, he picked up the plate, again with his teeth, and put it in the bowl in the sink. He turned on the tap awkwardly with a paw and left the plate to soak. He was back in his armchair when Dulcie came down the stairs with the tray of dirty tea things and a few biscuits that were left over. She stopped by Reggie and fed him the biscuits one at a time, smoothing his head while he demolished them, and then carried on into the kitchen with the tray.

The day wore on. He resisted the temptation to switch on the television. That would have caused a commotion and no mistake, he mused. Instead he lay there dog napping (so that's where they got it from) for the rest of the day and night.

Dulcie went to bed in the spare room and the house grew fairly quiet, that is as far as houses ever go quiet. Reggie was woken continually by odd creaks, clicks and scuttles which worried him until he realised what they were. Mice behind the skirting boards. He'd long suspected that they had mice but had never heard them before. Obviously his new dog ears were more sensitive than his human ones had been, opening up a new world of strange noises. He dozed fitfully between these starts, dreaming that he and Waldorf were being chased by blobs and fat men with little moustaches and lank hair.

Chapter Six

Monday the twelfth. It was growing light as Reggie awoke. Realisation came back to him and he opened his eyes and looked around in desperation. He lay there, thinking and puzzling furiously, but no solution sprang to mind. The call of nature was becoming insistent. There was no sound of movement from upstairs so, jumping quietly down from his armchair, he trotted off, unlocked the back door and performed his toilet over the drain, looking around constantly to see if he was being observed even though common sense told him that no one in his household would be up. He wasn't too sure about Dulcie. She might be an early bird, although she didn't look it.

After hosing down the yard he went back inside to see what he could steal for breakfast, though how he could steal from himself was a bit of a puzzle. Opening the fridge he gazed mournfully at the cheese. He fancied that with some biscuits but if he started it he would have to finish it, as there was no way that great big teeth marks could be left on the remains.

There were packets of unopened biscuits in the bottom of a cupboard so he picked up a couple and, again using his teeth, he tore them open and ate the lot, scrumping up the packets and putting them in the pedal bin. Using his tail he swept the crumbs under the cooker. After letting himself out once again, he had a drink of water from the tap in the yard and then made his way back up to High Tor. He had no clear idea in mind, except that he didn't know what else to do, and any activity was better than hanging around moping.

He met no one on his journey and, arriving at the spot where he and Waldorf had been slugged or drugged and generally messed about with, he searched until he found the place where he had been standing when he found his peephole.

There they were. His old human footprints. Just as he had cut them out of the ground the night before last. He stood on his hind legs, pawing the air, but knew that his eyes were at least a foot below where they needed to be. And anyway, he couldn't keep still long enough to focus them because he was wobbling to and fro trying to keep his balance. He dropped back on all fours and wandered down into the bracken. The shape of the depression made by the spaceship still showed, but here and there a springy twig or branch had thrust itself back into the air and he realised that it – whatever it was – was gone.

He sat and looked around him, feeling sick. Was he

condemned to be a dog for ever? He didn't think that he could face that prospect. And poor old Waldorf, strapped to a bed or in a straitjacket for the rest of his life. There had to be some way out of it, but what? What could he do? How could he tell anyone the predicament that he and Waldorf were in? If he figured out a way to communicate with humans, he would be looked on as a freak. He could be dognapped and wind up in a circus or sideshow.

He loped disconsolately home and found Lucy and Dulcie in the yard at the back staring at the pools of water that were still there from his morning's ablutions. He instinctively went to put his paw over his penis to hide it again, but stopped himself. No one ever took any notice of a dog's penis anyway.

'Well, I don't know what to make of it,' Lucy was saying. 'Someone has obviously been washing the yard down, but who, and why? It doesn't make sense especially at this time in the morning. And the empty biscuit packets . . .' She left the statement hanging in the air. Reggie rubbed up against her leg and she turned. 'And you, sir. Just where have you been this morning?' Turning to Dulcie she said, 'You didn't let Waldorf out, did you? Of course not, so how did he get out? Somebody has been here. Why didn't you bark or something, Waldorf?' She turned back towards the house. 'I'm going to phone Gus,' she said. 'There's something funny going on. We could have been murdered in our beds.' She made her way purposefully back indoors on trembling legs. Reggie and Dulcie followed her, waiting in the lounge while she phoned.

'He'll be right over,' Lucy announced a few minutes later. Turning to Reggie, who had climbed into his armchair, she said with impatience in her voice, 'Now come on, Waldorf, you know that Reggie doesn't like you climbing on his chair. Get off.' She watched as he slunk off the chair and flopped on the floor.

'In the basket,' she commanded. 'Go on, Waldorf, get in your basket, *now,*' and she slapped him on the rump so that he leapt up with surprise. Hanging his head he trotted quickly out to his too-small basket and tried to make himself comfortable.

Lucy went on, 'He's missing Reggie, I think, he's got that searching look on his face.' And she and Dulcie went into the kitchen to make the coffee.

'This is an unexpected twist,' thought Reggie. 'They'll look on me as being particularly useless now. That's the first time she has ever hit me.' He gave a croaky growl of misery that brought Lucy's and Dulcie's heads around the door to see what the noise was about.

He heard Gus's car pull up in the driveway and turned curiously to watch as Lucy let him in.

'Damned good housedog you've got there, ma'am,' he said with amusement, looking at Reggie sprawled out in the conservatory.

Lucy led him out to examine the evidence of the

empty packets and the still wet yard. 'Well, that's a puzzler,' he said, scratching his head. 'It's no good dusting for prints as you ladies were all over the place before you noticed anything.'

'I've just thought,' said Dulcie, 'there was that plate in the sink last night.'

'What do you mean?' asked Lucy. 'What plate in the sink?'

'That tea I brought up to you last night. When I poured the hot water out of the teapot that I had used to warm it, there was nothing in the sink that I can remember. Then when I came back down, there was a large plate in there. But I thought, oh well, it's me, not noticing it, so I just washed it up with the tea things and put it back on the dresser.'

Lucy looked concerned. 'Show me the plate,' she commanded, and the three of them trooped into the kitchen.

'This one.' Dulcie picked it up off the dresser and handed it to Lucy.

'This one?' repeated Lucy in amazement. 'But this is the one the ham was on.' She went over, opened the fridge and looked in. 'It's gone!' she exclaimed, and her face turned rather pale.

The three of them searched all over the house, looking under beds and in cupboards and even in the attic. Reggie lay in his basket looking bored. He would have liked to have been able to tell them how it had happened, but . . .

They came back down and Gus was speaking.

'Well, all I can say is make sure all the windows and doors are locked and keep Waldorf in but leave all the inside doors open so that he can charge about if there is an intruder.' He gave a half grin in Reggie's direction as he said it, plainly unimpressed by what he saw.

After seeing Gus off and double-checking all the door and window locks, the women left for the hospital and Reggie watched them go. Then, unlocking the back door with his teeth again, he wandered out into the yard. They'd probably be gone for hours, so he had plenty of time to think.

The sun was shining on the yard by Waldorf's kennel. Reggie stretched out on the warm concrete and gave himself over to pondering his present condition. He had always been a pessimist in normal life and now, it seemed circumstances only confirmed his pessimism. He lay there, wallowing in self-pity and frustration.

Pug, the dog from the house at the back, couldn't have picked a worse time to make an entrance through the fence. He made his way straight to Reggie with his usual snapping and snarling greeting. Reggie lay there watching him with half-closed eyes, fury beginning to build inside him. Natural self-confidence and a couple of years of successful Waldorf-baiting had left Pug unprepared for what was to come. Reggie sprang. A quick snap and his teeth were securely locked in the loose skin behind Pug's ear. Scrambling to his feet, with the howling Pug hanging from his jaws pawing the air in desperation, he stalked across on stiff legs to the water butt, which was full. Standing on his back legs he swung the screaming and frantically struggling animal over the top and into the water. Pug sank immediately and when he resurfaced, coughing and spluttering, Reggie pushed him under again. After the third ducking, Reggie decided his terrified victim had had enough, so he stood there watching as the quaking Pug got his front paws on the edge of the butt and, levering himself up and over the edge, landed in a sodden state on the floor. A growl and snarl from Reggie sent Pug hurtling off as if the very devil was after him, down the yard and through the hole in the back fence, howling fit to wake the whole village.

Reggie watched him go with some satisfaction and trotted back into the house. Reaching up, he turned the key in the back door with his teeth. Almost certainly there would be hell to pay when someone from the house at the back came round in a couple of minutes to complain about the condition of Pug. 'Bet he won't be back here in a hurry,' he thought gleefully.

He was right. Five minutes later there was a furious knocking at the front door, and taking a quick look Reggie could see Mrs Tait from the house at the back, looking most irate. She rang the bell and Reggie thought that perhaps he ought to act normally so he stood up against the front door and gave a deep bark. Pug, outside on the end of a lead, nearly had a heart attack. He tried to get away and almost pulled his owner over in his efforts. Reggie tried a couple more barks and snarls and Mrs Tait gave up. She tied Pug to the gatepost and after writing a note on a piece of paper produced from her bag she popped it through the letterbox. Reggie looked at it. It simply asked Lucy to phone her as soon as she could on an important matter, so Reggie left the note where it was and got back into his armchair for a snooze. Jason, meanwhile, was telling his mum what he had just seen next door. His mother looked at him.

'You saw what?' she said with amusement in her voice. 'Tell me again about Waldorf,' and she watched her small son as he went through what he had seen next door.

'Fantastic imagination,' she thought. 'Wait till I tell his dad.' She patted him on the head and gave him a loving hug and a biscuit out of the tin on the dresser.

Chapter Seven

At the hospital, a conference was taking place. If the doctors and consultants were completely stumped they were keeping it to themselves. After completing their tests early that morning, they had waited for Lucy to arrive with Dulcie and had questioned her for an hour about Reggie's actions prior to his disappearance. What had he had to eat? To drink? Any phone calls, letters, strange callers at the house?

'Clutching at straws,' as Dulcie told her husband later.

'Well, I think we'd better go and observe his reaction when he sees you,' one of the doctors said to Lucy, and they made their way to the ward where Waldorf was lying, still strapped in his bed.

When he saw Lucy, he went wild. He swung his head back and forth and horrible sounds issued from his lips, which dripped saliva. The bed rocked with his exertions and everybody stood back in horror. Lucy approached him and reached out her hand.

'Careful, Mrs Bagshott-Hawkes,' one of the doctors said, but Lucy ignored him and stroked Waldorf's head. His tongue came out in an attempt to lick her hand and even more whines and snuffles issued forth.

'Careful,' the doctor said again, grabbing her hand and pulling her back. 'He's having a fit. Surely it can't be rabies? He was with a dog, you say? We'll have to do more tests, I'm afraid. Nurse, you'd better use something to quieten him down or he'll be doing himself some damage.' He ushered them out into the corridor. Lucy was crying again, and Dulcie comforted her.

'Before you come down again you'd better phone me, I think,' said the doctor. 'Your presence seems to set him off.' He turned to Dulcie. 'Could you look after Mrs Bagshott-Hawkes and see that she gets home all right, and get someone to stay with her for a while?' Then he said his goodbyes, still assuring her that everybody was doing all they could to get Mr Bagshott-Hawkes back to normal, etc., etc.

Dulcie drove home, and as she swung her car into the drive Reggie got off his armchair to see if he could glean any news of Waldorf's progress, though he knew in his heart there would be none.

As they came in through the front door Dulcie picked up the note and handed it to Lucy, who glanced at it with a puzzled expression on her face.

'It's from Myra Tait,' she said, handing it to Dulcie. 'I wonder what she wants? Oh well, she can wait a minute till we've had a cup of tea.' She unpinned her hat and they both went out to the kitchen.

Reggie grinned sourly to himself. There was going to be another mystery to add to the others. He followed them into the kitchen hoping to learn something of what had gone on in the hospital, but could make no sense out of their monosyllabic conversation. He could see that both women were too subdued to talk much.

Lucy telephoned Mrs Tait and put the phone down in amazement. Dulcie looked at Lucy full of curiosity, seeing the look on her face.

'What was all that about?' she asked.

'Something about her dog coming home soaking wet and frightened nearly to death, but what it's got to do with me I don't know, I really don't. I could do with people keeping their problems to themselves just now.' She sank wearily into Reggie's armchair, dog hairs or no dog hairs.

Mrs Tait duly arrived looking tight-lipped and dragging a still damp Pug up the drive to the front door. Reggie, sprawled in his basket in the conservatory, decided to keep out of the way and be quiet. The situation was going to get complicated enough without Pug having a fit when he saw him. Lucy opened the front door and greeted Mrs Tait, glancing at Pug with little enthusiasm.

'Hello,' she said warily. 'Perhaps you had better leave Pug outside as Waldorf is loose in the house. Although normally he's very good with other dogs.'

'Look,' said Myra Tait vehemently, wasting no time on social niceties, 'someone has tried to drown him. Frightened to death. Scarred him for life.' Scooping Pug into her arms, ignoring Lucy's suggestion to leave him outside, she swept into the house clearly ready for a fight. 'Someone must have heard the noise poor old Pug made. I'll have 'em in court, I will.'

'We've only just come in, from the hospital, seeing poor old Reggie,' said Dulcie. 'There's been no one here.'

Lucy's eyes filled with tears again and she sat down with a bump. Myra Tait's manner softened.

'What's the matter with him?'

'Don't know,' said Dulcie, looking at Lucy who was now quietly weeping into her handkerchief. 'He was rushed in last night.'

Myra looked uncomfortable. 'Well, something's been going on while you've been gone,' she said. 'I think you ought to go out there and see if anything is missing.'

'Let's all go and look,' said Lucy getting up out of her chair, glad to be doing something.

Out in the yard, the evidence was all too plain. The water level in the butt was down about four inches and there were scratch marks on the rim where a frantic Pug had clawed for a grip. The remains of the trail the drenched dog had left as he made his way towards the hole in the fence were all too visible.

'Don't touch anything,' warned Lucy. 'I'm going to phone Gus again.' She went back into the house and as soon as she was out of earshot Myra turned to Dulcie.

'What's going on?' she whispered.

'Oh, I expect it's all entirely innocent,' said Dulcie with an airy wave of the hand, 'but we don't know.' She gave a brief summary of the weekend's events to Myra, whose eyes widened in amazement.

When Gus turned up, he had a look at Pug and remarked on the bloody marks at the back of his neck.

'How did he get those?' he asked Myra as he examined the still-trembling dog.

'I don't know, that's how he came home,' said Myra. 'It happened over here somehow.' She looked defensively at the other two women. Gus walked around the back and took in the water butt and the mess on the floor.

'There's no chance he could have jumped in?' It was a combination of question and statement. The three women looked at him in disdain.

'He's a dog, not a bloody acrobat,' commented Myra acerbically. They walked around the yard again, looking for anything that would give them a clue to the goings-on, but there was nothing, so Gus wrote something in his book and said his goodbyes. The three women stood in the drive and watched him go.

'There goes a man as mystified as we are,' said Dulcie. Lucy turned to her.

'It's all connected somehow,' she said. 'This thing with Reggie and what's been happening in this house. I know I shouldn't say this, being a regular church-goer, but do you think that some poltergeist or spirit has invaded the house and caused all this to happen?' She looked around at the familiar trappings of her home with a worried look on her face.

Myra Tait said briskly, 'I wouldn't think so at all. I don't believe in all that bloody mumbo-jumbo.' Never one to mince her words, was Myra. 'There must be a rational explanation to all this, but we just can't see it at the moment.' She turned and untied Pug, who pulled away eagerly, throwing Myra off balance. She let go of the lead and Pug was off down the road like a bat out of hell, trying to put as much distance between himself and Waldorf's residence as possible.

Reggie in his basket had watched the proceedings with interest. He would have to be more careful. He lay there thinking.

What on earth could he do?

He put himself in Lucy's position. How would he have felt if one day Waldorf had started talking to him, telling him that he was Lucy, while at the same time Lucy was in hospital, completely out of her mind?

He heard the doctor come in and eavesdropped on the ensuing conversation. News of Waldorf in the hospital was 'No news'. No change, except that one of the male nurses had been bitten and had had a jab for rabies. Reggie stifled a chuckle and they all looked around at him.

'Poor old Waldorf,' said Lucy, 'that was his stomach rolling. Gosh, he's had nothing to eat, poor lamb.' Going to the kitchen, she opened a tin of Waldorf's favourite Meaty Chunks and put it in his tin dish which was on the floor by the basket. Reggie eyed it sourly, his stomach turning over in disgust. The glutinous mess was moving before his eyes, the piled meat chunks in their gravy gravitating slowly downwards like miniature slimy brown icebergs. He turned his head away to avoid looking at it.

'Now come on, Waldorf,' said Lucy, leaning over and pushing the tin dish to the side of his head. Reggie got to his feet and lumbered off to his favourite armchair where he stretched out, making sure that he was lying on his stomach.

'Now don't tell me *he* is going to be sick as well!' exclaimed Lucy with almost a wail in her voice. 'That will be the last straw. You know what he's like, Dulcie, when he sees food. Now look at him.' She leaned over and stroked Reggie's head. Reggie lay there, loving her touch. Lucy went on, 'I'll have to get the vet to him if he's ill. Whatever's going to happen next?' She turned away despondently. 'If he doesn't eat his food by the morning, I'll phone the vet before we go to the hospital.'

Reggie couldn't bear to see Lucy so upset, and anyway, he was feeling decidedly hungry. There was nothing else for it. Getting down from his chair he wandered back into the conservatory and went over to the dish. With a mighty effort he closed his eyes and scoffed the lot, and it went down much more easily than he'd thought it would. His drinking bowl was full of clean water and he lapped at it to wash away the taste, making a terrible mess with his unpractised drinking. With his stomach making horrible gurgling noises, he wandered to the back door and, even though he could have opened it himself, gave a howl for someone to come and open it for him, just like Waldorf used to if he'd been waiting for too long.

He looked out when they opened the door. 'Damn,' he thought to himself, 'it's started raining.' But he realised that, just like Waldorf, he would have to go out, so he bent his head down and, cursing to himself, stepped out into the rain which was now hammering down. 'At any rate,' he thought, 'I can go to the toilet and use the hosepipe in this weather and no one will be any the wiser,' but all the same he trotted off out of the gate and down the road.

He used a field screened by a hedge as a toilet

and, feeling more comfortable, continued off up to High Tor, more in desperation than for any other reason. He sat on the rim looking across the now dark depression with the rain pouring down, searching for some movement or flashing light that would give him a clue as to what was going on, but there was nothing, just the hiss of the rain and the creaking of the branches of the trees. He shivered and was making his way back down towards home when he saw a figure dressed for the weather, walking up the lane towards him. He dived into the hedge at the side of the lane and waited for the figure to pass by. It was Daft Jim. What was he doing out on a night like this? He heard Jim whistling to himself and stayed still until he had passed around a bend in the road and was out of sight.

Back on the lane, Reggie continued his journey home, arriving soaking wet. He howled outside the back door until Lucy appeared, carrying the old towel that they used to rub Waldorf down when he came home wet. Lucy rubbed him dry and he was sorry when she had finished and told him, 'Get in that basket, Waldorf.' But to show her that he was behaving himself, and because he didn't want her to worry more than she already was, he ambled over to the basket and, with a sigh that was as near to Waldorf's as he could make it, climbed in.

He saw that his dirty dinner things had been taken away and cleaned, and settled down in the basket, gradually drying off and dozing fitfully. Only when the two women were in bed did he get up and go to his armchair, where he settled down to sleep and prayed to himself that he could find some solution to his predicament in the morning.

Chapter Eight

Glenda Marsh arrived at the glass front door of Wharfman's insurance office in Merton Stow a few minutes before nine o'clock and saw a large amount of mail lying on the floor just inside.

'Unusual,' she thought.

Taking out her keys she let herself in, picked up the mail and put it on the counter. She walked through the door at the rear of the office and tapped on Reggie's door. No answer. She heard the front door opening and looked out. The rest of the staff were arriving.

'His nibs hasn't come in yet,' she informed them.

'Having a lie in, I expect.' This from Brenda. 'Probably had too good a weekend.'

Samantha Smith shook her head. 'Not 'im,' she said emphatically. ''E'd come to work if he was dying. Can you imagine 'im letting a party stop 'im coming to work? Come to that, can you imagine 'im 'aving a party?' She shook her head again. 'Bet 'e's broken down on the way in or something.'

When the phone went half an hour later with

the news that Reggie was in hospital, there was an unusual sense of loss.

'Told you there was something up,' said Sam, 'had to be pretty serious to keep 'im away. What's 'e done? Had an accident?'

'Lost his memory,' said Glenda. 'Found him wandering around with his dog by all accounts. Rufus!' She directed her shout down the corridor. 'Put the kettle on. Let's have a nice cup of coffee.'

The phone went again and Glenda was all wide-eyed and open-mouthed when she finished speaking.

'You'll never guess!' she said, almost breathless. 'That was a reporter from the *Merton Stow Clarion*. Wanted to know if our Mr Bagshott-Hawkes has been acting funny lately. Seems that they found him yesterday with his dog, starkers on the top of a mountain.'

'On the top of a mountain? Starkers? You mean . . . er . . . naked?' Brenda was trying to be delicate. 'What was he doing on top of a mountain?'

'Communicating with nature by the sound of it,' said Sam. 'And with the dog. Kinky, I call it. I've heard of these blokes before. Bunch of pervs.'

'That's not very nice, Sam,' said Brenda. 'He's never seemed kinky to me.' She looked at Sam with speculation.

'Well,' said Sam straight-faced, 'it's the quiet ones you've got to watch. That Rufus is another one if you ask me.'

'Come on, Sam . . . Rufus . . . Penny short of a pound, maybe, but a . . .'

'They've got photos anyway,' said Glenda. 'Seems he was cut to pieces. Blood all over.'

'There you are,' said Sam, 'some sort of perv ceremony that went wrong.' She went back to pounding her typewriter.

'They're coming here to interview us,' said Glenda. 'Get our pictures in the paper. Bit of free publicity for the firm. The bosses will be pleased. *The bosses*! Gosh, I'll have to phone them and tell them what's happening.'

'They won't be very happy if they think that their manager – ex-manager – was a perv,' said Sam determinedly.

'Shut up, Sam,' snapped Glenda. 'You'd better get down to some work. We don't want the big bosses coming in here thinking that we can't run this place and putting someone else in charge, now do we?'

The office soon clicked back into gear.

Chapter Nine

Tuesday dawned grey and murky. Bursts of rain scudded across the countryside and the conservatory howled as the wind found the smallest crack and whistled through it. Reggie lay in his basket and listened to the noise as a particularly heavy squall of rain hit the windows, threatening to blow the flimsy building off its foundations. Lucy and Dulcie were having breakfast in the dining room. The cheerful flames of the gas fire spread a glow through the room and in addition the central heating made the whole house warm and comfortable.

Reggie got up off his basket, wandered into the dining room and flopped down in front of the fire as he had so often seen Waldorf do. Only this morning, he thought grimly and with a twinge of conscience that was unusual for him, there was no one there to scoot him out into the uncomfortable conservatory. He lay on the sheepskin rug in front of the fire listening. Lucy was speaking.

'I know they said to phone first, but I'm going to the hospital anyway. Are you coming with me?'

Dulcie nodded. 'Of course I am,' she said. 'I agree with you, Lucy. These doctors don't know everything, and I should know, being married to one all these years.' She stood up and started to clear the table.

Reggie stayed where he was, luxuriating in the warmth of the fire until Lucy came back in and turned it off, so he went and lay down under the radiator in the hall. His head ached with worrying about his situation. He was glad that Lucy and Dulcie were going to the hospital. It showed that they were suspicious and that nothing seemed right.

The two women arrived at the hospital and walked unannounced up to the ward and the private room where Waldorf was lying. He was in bed with a drip in his arm and a tube carrying some form of liquid from a bottle on a stand into his nose. He was still wired up to a machine with a screen that glowed green and had lines of small blips running along it at intervals. There were some lines that had no blips on them and Lucy and Dulcie were still trying to take it all in when the doctor arrived. He examined the screen for a minute and then tore off the printed sheet of continuous graph paper that was spewing forth from the printer. He asked them to follow him and led them to his own office off the main corridor. He waved the graph paper at Lucy.

'You know what this is, Mrs Bagshott-Hawkes?'

he said. She shook her head. 'Well,' he continued, 'our difficulty is that certain parts of your husband's brain don't appear to be working. We have him on drips because he seems to have forgotten how to use a knife and fork, so we are feeding him intravenously. Quite frankly we don't know what is the matter with him. He doesn't seem to have had a knock on the head. We've had him X-rayed but can find nothing to account for it. We have been in touch with every hospital in the country to try to find a similar case, but haven't turned anything up at all as yet. Still, it's early days, and we are going to continue profiling. What I *can* tell you is that he mustn't be moved, except perhaps to go to another hospital. What we would like you to do is to write down anything and everything that has happened to Mr Bagshott-Hawkes over the past week, however trivial it may seem to you. Enquire around amongst his acquaintances, they may have noticed something.' He stopped and looked at them. 'It's always worst for the nearest and dearest. When people are in the state that Mr Bagshott-Hawkes is in now, they are out of it. It's their loved ones who suffer. I'm sorry that I have no good news for you, but as I said, it's early days as yet.'

Lucy and Dulcie sat in the car in the hospital car park and Lucy stared unseeingly straight ahead. Dulcie gave her a glance as she started up the car and headed out into the traffic. 'Poor Lucy, is this better or worse than a loved one dying?' she wondered as she threaded the car through the traffic jam and headed for home. 'At least, horrible as it sounds, if a person is dead then all the uncertainties disappear and one knows where one is. But this, this is worse. At least when someone dies, everything is taken off one's hands and one floats along on a tide controlled by a funeral director and the clergy. But this . . . being left in limbo . . .'

Reggie watched them come in, subdued. He might as well not be there for all the notice they took of him. The only comfort that he found in it was that it showed the extent of Lucy's love for him, Reggie. He lurched to his feet and followed the women into the lounge, putting his head in Lucy's lap as she sat in one of the big armchairs. Absently she patted him and fondled his ears, but it was only a reflex action. Dulcie made some tea and they were drinking it when there was a knock at the door. Dulcie went to see who it was.

'It's Jim Contrell,' she said when she came back into the lounge. 'He says that he wants to see you about Waldorf.' She glanced at Reggie, still sitting there in bliss.

Dulcie ushered in Daft Jim. Lucy stared at him. She knew Jim well – at least, she knew the old Jim – because she was a good friend of Sophia his mother. But apart from Saturday night, about which she could remember little, she hadn't seen this member of the

Contrell family since his transformation. She couldn't get over the difference in him.

'Jim,' she said. 'And what can I do for you?'

'Hello, Mrs Bagshott-Hawkes. It's nice to see you again, though not in these circumstances. I've come about Waldorf, as I told Mrs Nicholas.' He glanced at Dulcie, who twitched in wonder that he knew her name. 'I was thinking. Who is going to take him for walks now that Mr Bagshott-Hawkes is not very well? Well, I thought, why can't I take him? I've got nothing to do all day and it'll be nice for both of us to get out. He's a big dog and needs lots of exercise – not particularly in this weather, though.' He looked out of the window at the rain lashing down.

Lucy nodded her head in agreement and thanked him, saying yes, she would be grateful and Waldorf was such a gentle old dog even though he was so big. Yet at the same time she was remembering snippets of the breakfast conversation she'd had with Reggie a couple of days ago (was that all it was?) about Daft Jim's miraculous cure. He'd also told her how Waldorf had run off when Daft Jim approached him. Yet now there he was standing right next to the man without so much as a snarl or a raising of the hackles. The feeling of unreality came over her again.

Jim left after a few more minutes of light conversation saying that he would phone tomorrow, early, come rain or shine. Reggie watched him go. He really didn't want to go for a walk. *He was not a dog.* Would he be expected to go chasing after rabbits as the real Waldorf did? Well, hard luck, the rabbits could live in total security as long as he was about. What was it with this Daft Jim? (He would have to stop calling him that.) Sure, when he used to take Waldorf into the pub and Jim was there, before he had his cure and Waldorf's attitude changed, he had on occasion come over and made a fuss of the dog, much to Reggie's embarrassment. But now, now that he was 'normal', he should act normal and normal grown people didn't take somebody else's dog for a walk.

The day passed quickly enough. Dulcie went home to see how things were in her own house and a steady stream of visitors, all women, came and went, bringing cards and flowers and listening in shocked silence as Lucy repeated the story of what had happened. Reggie observed all the fuss with cool detachment. He was a nine-day wonder. He had often wondered how it would feel to be the centre of attention. He recognised the disaster syndrome in a lot of the visitors. The whole situation was much more exciting because there was no explanation for the course of events leading up to the supposed Reggie being in hospital.

The day slid into evening and after a call to the hospital to see if there was any change in the patient's condition, Lucy and Dulcie settled down in front of the television. There were a couple of soap operas that both women watched with avid interest and then the evening film came on, all about aliens invading the earth and enslaving people. Reggie perked up and paid attention. It was nothing like that at all, was it? He was studying it with critical interest when the women changed stations and he gave a little whimper of annoyance, but they just looked at him curiously then turned their eyes back to the box. He sloped off and settled on the rug in front of the fire where he dozed fitfully and dreamed the nightmare of the blobs and moaned and growled in his sleep until Lucy prodded him with her toe and made him move. He slept on the sheepskin rug that night, listening to the storm abating, and when morning dawned it was with an almost clear sky. He had his breakfast of biscuits and a drink of water and the smell of coffee and the bacon and eggs that were being eaten, with too much gusto for his liking, nearly drove him mad. As the women chatted easily at the breakfast table he sensed that Reggie, in the hospital, was drifting slowly to the back of their minds.

The telephone interrupted breakfast. It was Jim Contrell telling them that he would be there in half an hour if that was all right with them. Lucy said, 'Fine, I'll have him ready for you,' and went back to finish her breakfast. Reggie looked out of the window. He didn't want to go for any walk. It looked far too nippy out there and there were puddles of water lying about that would make his feet and legs soaking wet. He could see no enjoyment in that for a start, but there would be no getting out of it. He could tell Lucy was relieved that someone was taking the trouble to see to Waldorf's needs. The real Waldorf would have needed taking out and Lucy was acutely aware of that, but she had ignored the thought because she had too much to think about already without worrying about a dog, even one as lovable as Waldorf.

Jim arrived looking dressed for the weather in a warm parka that would keep out the worst of it, thick trousers and waterproof hiking boots, all new. Reggie looked at him sourly. Where was his warm extra coat and leggings and all? No, he was expected to leave this warm house and go traipsing about over the wet countryside just as he was. He recognised the futility of whining about it as that would be out of character for Waldorf, who would have been bounding about with joy at the very sight of the lead. Jim said to Lucy, 'Oh, by the way, Mrs Bagshott-Hawkes, I meant to ask you last night but it slipped my mind. Would it be all right for me to go and see Reggie in the hospital? I might be able to jog his memory a little and perhaps help in his recovery – that's if you don't mind, of course.' Lucy thought about it for a moment and then said no, she didn't mind. Anything to help get Reggie back to normal. She would have a word with the nursing staff when she went down there today. Jim thanked her and, saying 'Come on, boy' to Reggie, slipped out of the front door. Reggie looked at Jim with a warm feeling in his stomach. The man must have felt a lot more friendly to him than he had ever realised. They went out of the front gate and turned right, 'Up towards High Tor,' thought Reggie, quickening his pace and avoiding the puddles.

'Aha,' exclaimed Jim, 'I thought that you would take an interest soon.'

Reggie heard the remark and took it to mean that once he got used to being out with Jim, his interest would quicken. 'So be it,' he thought, and pulled strongly ahead so that he could try to dictate which way they would be going; all the way up to High Tor, if he had his way. There was no opposition on Jim's part. He seemed content to come along for the walk and even unclipped the lead off Reggie's collar. Reggie sensed that Jim would follow wherever he went so he stopped wearing himself out and settled down to a steady pace. In no time at all they arrived at the spot where it had all gone wrong for Reggie and Waldorf. He cast about until he found his cut-out footprints and stood on his back legs trying to find his peephole, but knew he was wasting his time. He sat down depressed and turned to look at Jim who was watching him with a quizzical expression on his face.

'So this is where it all happened, eh, Reggie?'

Reggie froze. He couldn't believe what he had just heard. Stock-still he stared at Jim. Daft Jim had called him Reggie. Why was that? Was it some association of ideas or what? But he had said 'This is where it all happened,' hadn't he? Please say it again, his look implored. Jim obliged.

'I said "So this is where it all happened, eh, Reggie?"'

Jim took the hood off his parka, placed it on a tree stump and sat on it. Reggie too sat down suddenly with a bump; all the strength seemed to go out of his legs.

Jim went on: 'I've know about it from just after they did it to you. When they swapped your brain for Waldorf's, I mean. I was experimented on before you; well, not exactly experimented. More that they had a look in my head and saw what was wrong and fixed it. I still am being used as a guinea pig in a way. They've made me the go-between to protect the pair of you and to intervene if things get out of hand, and I have to make sure that you both arrive back here in time for the change-over when you'll both have your brains put back in your proper bodies. They're as nutty as our lot experimenting on animals. That's what they've done to you. Just seeing if a brain can be swapped around. Like Dr Frankenstein. Think they're God. Like growing human ears on the backs of poor bloody rats. If you'd've invented a story like that a few years ago, they'd've put you in a lunatic asylum a bit bloody rapid, but there they are, doing it. These aliens are no different in their thinking than the human animal.

'Don't get me wrong, I am grateful to them for what they've done to me. They've changed my life completely, and for the better, but what they've done to you is diabolical and I told them so . . . They just appeared in front of me on Sunday morning. Seemed to slide out of a slit in the air somehow.

'They didn't take any notice of me slagging them off, just assured me that you would be all right in the end, provided we get you and Waldorf back here on Sunday afternoon at three o'clock. They're leaving this planet then; going off somewhere else, God knows where, so we can't miss them, whatever we do, because they won't be back for ten years. They don't speak to me as such, you know. Not in words, that is. The one who was staring at me seemed to have the conversation with me in my head. God knows how.'

Reggie felt helpless. He wished that he could communicate with Jim like that. He gazed dolefully at his companion and wagged his tail in a half-hearted fashion, much as he had seen Waldorf do. Jim seemed to read his thoughts.

'If you understand me, nod your head. If not, shake it. All right, Reggie?' He rubbed Reggie's ears in a friendly fashion that sent shivers running up and down Reggie's spine at the thought that here was an ally, a much-needed friend.

For someone who had never had a close friend and who had looked upon friendship as a prop for those who could not or would not be self sufficient, this lifeline being proffered by someone he had looked down on – or even worse, someone he thought should have been put down at birth – proved almost too much to bear. His heart thumped and pounded and he thought of the irony of it if he had a heart attack now, just as things were beginning to look a little less grey. But then he wasn't in his fat old body . . . no . . . he was in Waldorf's, and Waldorf's heart was a healthy one (he hoped).

Just when he had thought that he was alone in the world with his problem, help had turned up from the most unlikely source. He looked up and nodded his head vigorously at Jim and Jim laughed with delight.

'Now,' he said, 'you are a dog to everyone except me, so act like one. I'll need your help to get Waldorf out of the hospital. You're the only one I can trust. You know the score. Everybody thinks that it's you in that bed and that you have lost your marbles. If I was to go in there, with people knowing my past as the village idiot, and tell them that the object lying in their bed is really Waldorf, and that the great hairy thing trotting alongside me is Reggie Bagshott-Hawkes, they'd have me in a straitjacket as quick as a shot. Or maybe they'd just chuck me out of the hospital and make sure that I was kept well away from Waldorf in future. Either way, that would be the end of it for you and him, and while I would stand by you and treat you as Reggie, no one else would. You could look forward to spending the rest of your life as Waldorf.'

He stopped. A great shudder ran through Reggie as he realised fully the enormity of what Jim had told him. No way must they miss their assignment in five days' time. Spend the rest of his life like this? What would the rest of his life *be* anyway? Waldorf was four now, so that left ten years at the outside, and old dogs usually went blind and became incontinent and had to be put down. *Put down*. The hair stood up all along his back and his bowels moved at the thought. For God's sake, they mustn't fail.

Jim stood up. 'Come on,' he said, 'let's have a look round and see what we can come up with.' He started off walking around the edge of the depression.

'What we are looking for,' he said as they trudged around, 'is somewhere out of sight and sheltered if possible where we can bring Waldorf and wait. Once you're inside the spaceship you'll be safe, as they put this warp thing out that somehow diverts people's gaze away, but we'll have to hide for a while before they arrive. Make no mistake about it, we're going to have to kidnap Waldorf.' Reggie stopped in his tracks. Christ, they electrocuted people in the States for that; and over here . . . twenty years. He caught up with Jim who was still outlining his plan.

'When they find out that he's vanished from the

hospital, all hell is going to break loose. He's classified as dangerous now, because he's already bitten a couple of the staff. They'll be out in force looking for him.' He stopped and addressed Reggie.

'Another thing, he'll only be wearing a hospital nightshirt so we will have to have blankets to wrap him in to keep him warm while we're waiting.' He laughed. 'Of course, you realise that you will only be wearing the nightshirt when they find you, don't you? But you'll probably think that that's a small price to pay for returning to normal. Hope you don't catch pneumonia in the process, though. It'd be awful for you to snuff it after all that we'll be going through.' He laughed again and slapped his thigh.

Reggie scowled. Jim was too flippant by half. Reminded him of one of his staff. Never serious enough, but he couldn't fault his work. He hoped that Jim was the same; God how he hoped. Well, Jim was his only chance, that is if this wasn't some long-running nightmare that he was having. He would have to grasp the opportunity with both hands, or paws, he thought with a wry grin, which contorted his face something terrible.

He loped after Jim who had begun casting about through the tall wet grass. He wished that he had Waldorf's memory at the moment, as Waldorf had criss-crossed this area dozens of times and probably knew every rabbit track and mole hill in there. They kept out of the depression itself because, as Jim said, 'You wouldn't want to be in there when a couple of hundred tons of spaceship landed, now would you?'

They came across the remains of an old hut. No roof, just standing walls and a square hole where the window used to be. The grass and brushwood inside was as tall and well grown as that outside. Jim shook his head.

'Not what we want at all,' he said. 'They'll see this and look in. It's too obvious. What we want is something that blends into the landscape that they'll walk right by. Something innocent-looking.'

It was Reggie who found what they were looking for. Following a narrow track between the overgrown blackberry bushes, he almost fell down a large crack in the ground where at some time in the past the earth had started to slip down the side of the steep depression. He pushed his way back out of the bushes and gave a howl and Jim struggled over to see what all the noise was about.

The crack ran back into the hill at an angle, only about three feet at its deepest, but the brambles, cascading down over the entrance, effectively concealed it from anyone looking down from the top, or from anywhere else for that matter.

'Good boy, Reggie,' said Jim, patting him on the head again. 'Now we must be careful getting out as we don't want to leave a trail and advertise the fact that someone has been here.' He eased himself out, trying not to disturb the long grasses and thorny shoots that acted as cover. Reggie went out the other way; following the narrow track that had been made by rabbits and taking one of the divisions in the path that led upwards, he gained the rim some way to the left of Jim who was waiting for him at the top.

They made their way back to the place where the footprints were cut in the ground and Jim took out his parka hood and put it back on top of the stump he had been sitting on before.

He looked back at the place where the crack in the ground was. There was no hint of it being there at all. He walked back a few paces, still looking, and nodded his head in satisfaction.

'Perfect.' He went back and sat on the stump, addressing Reggie who had been watching him quizzically.

'Reggie, old son, I think we've cracked it. At least, I mean that we've sorted out the hiding place, but really that's the easy bit. Getting him out of the hospital and up here is the hard bit.' He sat there in contemplative silence.

Reggie felt useless. He knew that he couldn't be much help. All the conversation was one way, from Jim to him, and all he could do was nod or shake his head and pray that Jim would ask him the right questions in the right way. Questions that demanded a 'Yes' or 'No' answer. Jim stood up.

'Come on,' he said, 'I'd better take you back, and then later on I'll go and have a look round the hospital, see what I can come up with.' He started off down the hill to the lane, Reggie trotting alongside him, bursting with questions.

How was Jim going to get to the hospital? It was twelve miles away and he would have to go by bus; he didn't think Jim could drive. Panic rose in him again. How were they going to kidnap Waldorf and spirit him away on a bus? The very idea was ridiculous.

They went back down the lane to Merton Minor, each preoccupied with his own thoughts. There was no one in at Reggie's, so they made their way to Jim's house which smelled of baking and exuded an air of welcome, comfort and warmth.

Jim's mother was there taking trays of fairy cakes out of the oven and knocking them out on to wire racks on the big kitchen table that stood in the middle of the room. Jim pinched one of the cakes and, breaking it in half, gave a piece to Reggie and ate the rest himself. His mother flipped him playfully across the ear with the admonition, 'Leave those cakes alone, they're for tea.' She looked at Reggie, licking his lips to savour the taste of the small treat he had just had.

'Lord, he's a big 'un and no mistake,' she said. 'If he bit anyone, he'd have 'em in half with those teeth.' She turned to take some more trays out of the large oven. Jim went out through the back door, motioning for Reggie to follow, and they made their way out of the back gate into the field. There was a large tractor inside a shed and Jim climbed on it and started it up.

'Go and stand over there, Reggie,' he shouted over the noise of the engine, indicating with his hand the side of the house some ten yards away. 'I've never driven anything before so I'll need to have a bit of room to get used to it. I know how it works because I've watched Len drive it and the car, but I'll have to practise before I go out on the road.' So saying he put the gear lever in where he thought reverse gear was and backed out of the shed in a series of jumps and stops that brought Reggie's heart into his mouth for fear that Jim was going to kill himself and so condemn him, Reggie, to permanent doggishness. Anyway, he failed to see how a tractor would help in the plan to kidnap Waldorf. He gave a mournful howl in protest and Jim's mother came rushing out of the back gate to see what all the noise was about. She watched blankly as Jim started forward again, then stopped and went into reverse.

'What are you doing?' she asked when he finally stopped and clambered off the machine.

'Learning to drive this thing, of course,' said Jim, grabbing hold of her and swinging her off her feet.

'Put me down, Jim,' she squealed, pushing at his shoulders. 'There, now you've got flour all over your new parka.' She squealed again as he gave her a bear hug before putting her down. 'You be careful, Jim,' she went on seriously. 'That's a powerful machine you've got there. They're not for playing with. I don't think Len would be very happy if he saw what you were up to, he'd be worried sick. Better leave it till he comes home and get him to show you how it works, that's safest.' Then she hurried back into the house muttering that her cakes would be burning.

'I think she's right,' said Jim to Reggie, and they went out of the field by the side gate, back to Reggie's house. There was still no one in so they went around to the back and Jim clipped Reggie to his chain by the kennel.

'Now don't forget, Reggie. Dog-like. No trying to act like a human, or you'll only confuse people and they'll start watching you too closely.' And he was off with a wave of his hand, back out of the drive and out of sight. Reggie watched him go and crept into his kennel, his mind buzzing with questions.

'Please God, let nothing happen to Jim,' buzzed through his mind like a dirge. It was warm in the kennel with the midday sun shining on it. Soon, in spite of himself, he fell into a nap. Jason, up in his tree, waited expectantly for something to happen. Nothing did.

Chapter Ten

Jim walked out of the driveway of The Elms, Reggie's house, with a jaunty step, aware of Reggie looking dumbly after him. But he didn't feel jaunty at all, he felt depressed and at a loss as to what to do next. 'They', those damned space invaders, had not foreseen, when they had started this experiment, that Waldorf was going to wind up in a hospital, immobile and helpless. What they had probably expected was that Waldorf would take on Reggie's persona by taking on his body, and vice versa.

'Damned crackers. Just like our lot. Bags of brains but no intelligence.'

The only good thing to have come out of all this was that he was 'normal', and it looked as if he would remain so.

He thought back again to the time when he realised he had changed; walking down High Tor to the gate at the bottom. His legs and body had suddenly gone weak, so that when he got to the bottom he had to lean against the fence for several minutes until he recovered. He had looked at his hands and generally examined himself. Familiar but unfamiliar. His mind went back to . . . to before this happened. Before *what* happened? He had looked around and the day seemed the same as his last memory of it. Where was that? The field behind his house. He felt in his pockets. Handkerchief. Piece of string. Couple of pebbles.

His mind flipped back over the years. The schooling. Special schooling. His fellow pupils. Something wrong with all of them. *I am the same as you* his brain screamed at him. His teachers had been more like nurses.

He remembered conversations between his mother and father, brother and sisters, conversations that had not included him, though now and again remarks would be shouted at him in a different context to the conversations of the others.

He had pushed himself away from the fence and let himself out through the gate with exhilaration building up inside him. 'I'm different. Something has cured me,' he had told himself out loud, and hurried off down the hill and home to an unbelievable family reunion.

His mind returned to the scheme in hand. Reggie and Waldorf would be switched back, as long as they kept their appointment. Four days. They'd have to get Waldorf out of the hospital the night before or even on the morning of the switch. It would be too great a risk to have him at High Tor too long. Too great a risk of discovery and consequently missing the appointment – and a life of hell for both of them, especially Waldorf who would be strapped to his bed for ever more.

Reggie would get by. He wouldn't like it, but he had the brains to make the best of it, not like Waldorf, poor sod. Jim's shoulders slumped. How in the hell were they going to manage it?

He dared not ask his brother for help, for the simple reason that he would have to explain why he wanted assistance. Even if he could convince Len that what he was telling him was the truth, there was the complication that if they got caught, no one would believe them and they would both be charged with kidnapping and face a prison sentence. He supposed that the family would never forgive him if he landed his brother in prison on what would look like some bizarre whim.

He decided to walk down to the paper shop to get something to read while he waited for Lucy to arrive home with news from the hospital, but turned back as he saw her car turning into the drive. He hurried back to open the door for her, and noticed that she was much more composed than she had been yesterday. She was coming to terms with the situation in a normal human way.

'Thank you, Jim,' she said as she got out of the car. Dulcie, getting out the other side, nodded amiably at him.

'Hello, Jim,' she said.

'How's Reggie today?' he asked, having stopped himself just in time from saying 'Waldorf'.

'Just the same,' said Lucy, her face clouding over. 'I told the doctor that you would be calling in to see him and he thinks it's a good idea. Anything that might jog his memory is worth trying, he said, so you can pop in any time you like. He's in a private room so you won't be bothering the staff.'

'That's fine,' said Jim. 'I'll nip down there now, I think. By the way, I've tied Waldorf up to his kennel, and he seems happy enough, he had a good run. We understand each other, it seems, he's no trouble at all. I'll pick him up every day while Reggie's poorly if that's all right with you?' She nodded, and he handed her the lead, made his goodbyes and walked back down the drive.

'Well,' he thought, 'at least something's going right.' He walked on feeling much more optimistic.

He caught a bus to Merton Major and walked to the hospital, getting the lie of the land. He had of course been brought here often in his previous existence, but he couldn't remember the way the streets ran or which were the main roads, and he stopped frequently to ask directions. Finally he saw signs pointing the way to the hospital and soon found it just off the main road.

He walked in with the crowds of people, most of them carrying bunches of flowers or small packages.

There were so many people about that he realised that he must have arrived at the official visiting time. He buttonholed a man in a white coat pushing a wheelchair along a corridor and was directed back the way he'd come to a door with 'Enquiries' painted on it in gold. He went in and after a few minutes a pleasant young woman with large spectacles and a nice smile asked him if she could help him.

'Yes,' he said. 'A Mr Reggie Bagshott-Hawkes. I've come to see him but I don't know my way about this hospital, so if you could direct me . . . ?' He left the question hanging in the air while she consulted her lists.

'He's on the third floor,' she said. 'Walk back up the corridor to the lifts, he's in ward C3.'

He found the lifts in a large hall. There were six on either side, the ones on the right marked for hospital staff use only. Jim looked at one of those that stood empty and could see that it was much bigger than a normal lift. As he waited for his lift to arrive, two porters and a nurse came into the hall with a patient lying on a trolley and wheeled it into the open lift. Jim could see now why it was so big. His lift, which was only half the size, arrived and he took it to the third floor, following the signs to C3. He went through glass double doors that opened both ways and shut automatically behind him.

'Good afternoon,' he said pleasantly to a pretty

young nurse behind a desk. 'I've come to see Mr Bagshott-Hawkes. My name is Jim Contrell.'

She took him to a private room where Reggie's body lay in the bed.

'He's under sedation but if you want to talk to him, carry on. I'm told that he can probably hear you subconsciously and maybe it will be a comfort to him. If you want anything, don't be afraid to call me.'

Jim asked in a hushed voice how often they checked on him and the nurse said about once an hour. The doctors could turn up at any time, but had only been once today.

She left him and he looked over Waldorf with keen interest. He would have to take the drips out, disconnect the urine bottle and somehow get him off the bed and out of this room. He was going to be a dead weight, completely helpless. Jim looked out of the window and saw that a fire escape ran directly underneath it, with three flights of steps to negotiate from there to the ground. That would be out of the question with at least two hundred pounds on his back. He might be a changed person, but he wasn't Superman.

He went to the door and looked out carefully. Peering down the corridor he could not see the desk at all, but there was a large convex mirror angled up to the ceiling that would give the person sitting behind the desk a view along the passageway. There was a keyhole in the door but no key, either inside or out. Probably kept behind the desk on a board, he thought, but he could check that later. He went back into the room and shut the door quietly. It was a good fit and he had to push it firmly to make the latch click. He turned his attention to the window. It was old-fashioned, with small square panes and wooden shutters that looked as if they hadn't been used for years. He tried to pull them open and they creaked before moving a little. He thought that with a little oil on the hinges he might be able to get them fully across. The iron bar that acted as a lock was still in place on its pivot behind the leading left-hand shutter and it swung easily when he tried it. He pushed the shutters back and decided to explore the place a little further. The more he knew, the better able he would be to formulate a plan to get Waldorf out of there.

He walked back down the corridor to the desk.

'How can I help you?' asked the nurse.

'Well, actually I was wondering if there was a recreation room where he could go if he gets any better.'

She looked at him. 'There is a television room at the end, down there.' She pointed to the double doors at the opposite end of the corridor. 'But I don't think your friend will be in any condition to use it for some while.'

'Thank you,' said Jim, and turned away. The only keys he had seen were hanging at her hip, so that ruled out the idea of filching the one to the door of

Waldorf's room. He went back to Waldorf's bedside and sat there brooding over the problem. This was going to be a lot harder than he had thought. After a few fruitless minutes he left the room and went back to the nurse telling her that he was going but that he would call back from time to time to see if he could catch Mr Bagshott-Hawkes in a more conscious state.

'Any time, Mr Contrell,' she said. 'Any time.' He walked back to the lift hall where he waited for a while to see how many people were about and how everything worked.

He studied the board and discovered that the visiting times, for the normal wards, were from two till four in the afternoon but only for an hour in the evenings, from seven o'clock to eight. He decided that two till four on a Saturday afternoon would probably be the busiest time of all, when there would be lots of people milling about. He grinned wryly to himself as he realised that he was beginning to think like a crook. He wandered around the hospital, finding the porters' lodge with ranks of wheelchairs parked outside.

Then he walked around the grounds and the side streets outside the hospital, making mental notes as to how the traffic was parked and where would be the best place to have a vehicle stashed away. In the hospital grounds would be preferable, but from what he had just seen there was very little room for parking there, especially at visiting time.

He roamed around for hours, until he started to get confused, and finally sought a snack bar for a coffee and a hot dog, covered with tomato sauce – a habit from his former days. At quarter to seven he went back into the hospital and hung around in the lift hall on floor three, watching the people emerging from the lifts in ever-increasing numbers. Finally he came to a conclusion.

'So,' he mused, 'the best time to go down would be when the lifts are coming up full and going down empty, and there are a lot of people about.' He slipped into Waldorf's room unseen. Waldorf was still lying there. The only movements were the bubble in his drip and his chest moving rhythmically up and down as he breathed.

There was a DO NOT DISTURB sign hanging on a rubber sucker on the back of the door and he pulled the sucker off, moistened it and stuck it back on again. That would probably come in handy. He left the hospital, again unobserved, and made his way back to the bus stop.

On the way home on the bus he pulled out a note book and ballpoint that he had filched from Len's room and began jotting down notes about the various points that had occurred to him at the hospital. His writing was clumsy, a throwback to the days spent in the special school when they had tried to drum a modicum of common sense into him.

He had been amazed at the number of cars illegally

parked in the hospital grounds, and in the surrounding side streets cars were also parked nose to tail.

He hadn't yet decided whether Saturday afternoon or Sunday morning would be the best time. The hospital would be at its busiest on Saturday, but then he'd have to hide Waldorf overnight . . . But whatever he decided, he would have to arrive in plenty of time and park in the nearest side street on the same side as the hospital. As to a vehicle, the only one that he could drive and had access to was that blasted tractor. It was also the only vehicle, other than a motorbike, that could be driven with a learner's licence. But it only had one seat on it so where in the hell could he put Waldorf? He scratched his head thoughtfully. He would have to get Len to show him how to drive that tractor tomorrow. It was cutting it a bit fine to leave it any later.

He mulled over the plan that was beginning to form in his head. He'd have to buy some of the things he needed, but that was no trouble these days. Any damage that was done would have to be paid for by Reggie when he was better. He grinned to himself at the plan. It should work, at least the first part should. It was the next stage that was going to be difficult, when he was going to have to use the tractor. He pushed the thoughts to the back of his mind and enjoyed the rest of the journey home.

Lucy answered when he knocked at her door and she invited him in. Dulcie was nowhere to be seen.

Lucy had been drinking coffee and was sorting through some papers on the table when he came in. She offered him a cup.

Thanking her for the offer, he refused, saying that he had only called in to tell her that he had been to see Reggie and that there was no change according to the nurses. Lucy seemed resigned to this rather bleak news.

'I'm sorry to say this, Jim, but I've lost a lot of faith in doctors these last few days. They've still got a long way to go to understand how the body really works. I don't know what to do next. They've had specialists in, but they don't seem to know what's the matter. I hope you don't mind me asking this, but I feel I can talk to you because you have had personal experience, and you seem to remember how you were. Did you have any knowledge at that time that you were . . . odd . . . different? Did you ever say to yourself that you wanted to be normal, cured?'

Jim shook his head. 'No. I didn't know that there was anything wrong with me. It's only now that I realise what I missed. If you're thinking about Reggie, being in the hospital, he won't remember a thing about it, I can assure you on that point.' He took her hand and tried to instil in her the confidence that he had from knowing the truth; that there was nothing wrong with the real Reggie's brain, it was just in the wrong place. She looked at him, puzzled.

'Why are you so confident? Do you know something that I don't?'

'No,' he lied, meeting her gaze with difficulty. 'It's just a feeling I've got. How's Waldorf? Can I see him?' He took her look for permission granted and escaped by walking through to the back door.

Reggie heard him come out and rose to his feet, a ripple of excitement running through him.

'Hello, old son,' said Jim. 'Not stopping long, just to tell you to get some rest and build your strength up as we'll have a lot to do when it starts. Eat all your food up and I'll fill you in as we get nearer the time for us to act.' He fondled Reggie's ears as he was talking, then left and walked down the drive into the dusk.

Reggie watched him go. *Rest.* How could he rest with the knowledge that if they failed he would be using this kennel as a home for the rest of his life?

Jim hurried down to the pub, when he had finished his supper, to have a word with Len before chucking-out time, about driving lessons.

Len was astonished by Jim's request, and looked a little annoyed. The novelty of his brother's transformation was beginning to wear off, and the shedding of a responsibility, even though welcome, was a disruption with which the family hadn't, as yet, fully come to terms.

'Christ, Jim!' he said. 'Are you bloody mad?' He stopped in some confusion. 'Er, sorry, er, what I mean is, why don't you go to a driving school? And what's the bloody hurry? I've got work to go to in the morning and I don't want to be running around in that thing before I go. You know what I'm like in the mornings, no good at the best of times.'

If there was one thing that the new Jim could do, and do well, it was to twist people around his little finger, and this he proceeded to do, much to the amusement of Len's cronies in the bar.

'Please, Len,' he said. 'I have had a drive of it but I just want telling what the different things are for, how to put the trailer on and things like that. I've been offered a job of sorts and I must be able to drive a tractor to do it. Twenty minutes is all I ask. I know that you've been doing things for me all my life, but only this once more and I'll be able to manage things from now on.' As Len still looked uncertain, he went on, 'I'll buy you a drink. What are you having?' and he picked up Len's almost empty glass.

Len gave a laugh. 'Go on then, if it's so important, but only a half, seeing as I have to get up even earlier in the morning now.' A ripple of laughter ran around the bar.

Jim bought the drink and, waving goodnights all round, went home and straight to bed. He didn't want to be interrogated about the job he'd been offered; Len would be doing enough of that in the morning, once he came to.

The morning dawned grey and murky. Jim was

up well before his usual time to make tea and start cooking bacon and eggs for the family breakfast. He had a bright fire going by the time they all came down, and his mother was pleasantly surprised to have her breakfast put in front of her.

Len grinned ruefully at the earliness of the breakfast. He had been hoping that Jim's request of the night before was a passing whim that would disappear by morning's light, but he could see that that had been too much to hope for. Half an hour later they were on their way out of the house, dressed for the weather, and Jim was being initiated into the mysteries of starting and driving the tractor.

'Be careful,' warned Len as they trudged back into the warm house for another cup of tea before he went off to work. 'They can be a bit tricky, especially on sloping ground, so take it very easy until you get used to it. By the way, what is this job? Nothing that I've heard of around here.'

'Manson over the other side of Swiffield,' lied Jim. He'd heard that a man named Manson had just bought the farm and knew that Len didn't know him.

'How do you know him? Only just moved in from what I hear. Didn't take you long to get your feet wedged in the door.' With a further admonition to be careful Len finished his large mug of tea and was gone.

Jim helped his mother clear away the breakfast

things then washed and dried the dishes and put them away. Mrs Contrell still couldn't get used to not having to look after him. He smiled to himself as she watched him picking up the dishes, and after he had seated her in the chair by the fire, with yet another cup of tea, he asked her if he could borrow a couple of quid, as he had to get some things. She rummaged in her bag, brought out her purse and took out a ten pound note.

'You have that, Jim,' she said, handing it to him. 'It's a pleasure to be able to do this and know that you have your own mind to make up these days.' She pulled him towards her and hugged him tightly then pushed him away with tears in her eyes. 'Now you go on,' she said, 'go and do what you want to do.' Jim put his outdoor clothes back on and went out whistling, to see Reggie and put him in the picture.

When he knocked on the Bagshott-Hawkes' door, and was invited in, he found Lucy on her own, except that is for Reggie, who came up to him wagging Waldorf's tail like mad and making little growling noises.

'Well, you've made a conquest there,' said Lucy, looking with surprise at the fuss the dog was making over Jim who stroked Reggie's ears and gave him a good patting.

'Where's Mrs Nicholas?' he asked, looking about him.

'Oh, she's gone back to her own house today, Jim,

but she's coming back over later. Things have got to return to normal no matter how much we dislike it.' Lucy turned away.

Jim felt like blurting out the truth, but what would Lucy's reaction be if he told her that this ungainly monster now rubbing up against her leg was Reggie? She'd think that he had had a regression, and that he was a candidate for the funny farm again. No, it was better to carry on with what he was doing. That way, if anything went wrong, there would be no difference to the present circumstances, although he would have to go on looking after Reggie for the rest of his life.

'I thought that I would take Waldorf for a walk, Mrs Bagshott-Hawkes,' he said. 'I know it's a little bit damp out there, but I think he would enjoy it.' He looked at Reggie who trotted out into the hall and came back in with his lead in his mouth. Lucy looked at him with amazement.

'Well! He's never ever done that before,' she said. 'You must be having a very good influence on him.' She accompanied them to the door and watched them stroll off down the road with Waldorf neither pulling nor being pulled, as had so often been the case with Reggie. She went back in and telephoned the hospital to be told, 'No change. He's had a peaceful night and seems comfortable.'

She put the phone down and stared into space. What did they mean by a peaceful night? Drugged up to the eyebrows, she supposed. She had better get back to work and fill in the gaps left empty by Reggie's absence. A thought struck her. She picked up the phone and started dialling. She'd have a coffee morning, even though there was a Women's Institute meeting tonight. Get all her friends around. Better than hanging around moping.

Jim and Reggie walked out of the gate and made their way down to the newsagent's.

'I've worked out a plan,' said Jim, 'but you'll have to help me with it. It all depends on timing so I'll have to get you into the hospital somehow to show you the layout, and what I want you to do. You have to create a diversion so that I can smuggle him out in the confusion. If we do it right, they won't miss him for some time, and we'll have more of a chance to get him hidden.

'Now we're going into the shop to buy some instant glue and a newspaper, and then we're going to Merton Major on the bus to the hospital so I can show you the plan. This time, when you go in, you'll have to use the steps at the back of the lift hall. You have to do it silently and frighten no one, but it will be different when we do it for real. Do you understand what I'm talking about?' Reggie shook his head. 'Never mind, I'll show you when we get there. It sounds more complicated than it is.' They had reached the shop, and went in to buy the glue which was kept behind the till to prevent it being pinched by glue sniffers.

'Four tubes of instant glue?' said Mrs Giles. 'What on earth are you doing with that much?'

'Oh, I have to glue a piece of wood about as big as a table top to its frame, and I don't want to run out of glue half way through,' said Jim. 'And could I have a small tin of bike oil as well, please?'

'And how is Mr Bagshott-Hawkes?' she asked as she handed him the bag with the glue and oil in and took his money. Her conversation was stilted and awkward. Treating Jim as normal needed getting used to.

'About the same,' replied Jim, and after some more conversation of the same ilk they left the shop and trudged back up to the bus stop where they waited for the bus to town.

On the long avenue alongside the hospital grounds, large coniferous trees grew out of the pavement every few yards. They were old trees that had been planted too close together when they were saplings and now stood, shoulder to shoulder, with their branches growing into each other, forming an effective screen. In addition, the corner house on the main road had a long garden wall running back up the avenue for some sixty yards, so that anyone parking in the road outside the wall was out of sight of the houses running back up the road. It was a discreet parking place, but handy for the hospital.

When Jim and Reggie arrived there were already

some cars and vans parked there, and as they watched more arrived.

As the morning wore on, yet more cars arrived, most of their occupants appearing to go to the hospital, while some went to the shops which were around the other corner in the opposite direction. Jim and Reggie walked up and down the avenue noting the fact that every house had a driveway with a garage at the end.

'Now,' said Jim finally, 'we're going into the hospital. You walk about twenty yards behind me as though you're not with me. Watch me walk to the lift, then go up the stairs which will be to your right as we walk in. Go up three flights of stairs and you'll be on floor three. Come out into the lift hall and you'll see C3 over the door that I'll go through. Sit down and I'll wait till I see you and then I'll walk through the swing doors into the ward. Now these swing doors only need a push to open so you'll have no difficulty when you come to use them, OK? I'll come straight back out, because I don't want to see Waldorf, but if I'm spotted I'll have to go in and visit him and stay for about half an hour. If that happens, you go back to the avenue and wait for me.' With that they walked towards the front gate of the hospital with Reggie dutifully falling back twenty or so yards behind Jim, who walked past the porters' cabin and on up to the entrance to the lifts.

Reggie went through after him, creeping tight up

against the wall of the cabin so that he couldn't be seen, and found himself in the entrance hall. He saw Jim just stepping into one of the six lifts and, looking around to his right, saw the stairs going up. He bounded up, meeting no one, and sat in the hall waiting for Jim to arrive and lead the way to C3.

C3; it was over there as plain as a pikestaff. Jim stepped out of the lift, walked over to the door and, pushing it open, stepped through. Reggie turned and ran down the stairs, nearly knocking over a couple of young nurses giggling at something as they climbed up. Their giggles turned to screams as he appeared racing down towards them, and the noise frightened him so much that the hairs on his back rose which made him look even more ferocious. He forgot all about the back stairs that he was supposed to keep an eye out for and panicked; running out of the hospital and around the corner to the avenue where he sat, panting and trembling, until Jim arrived and looked at him in amusement.

'I heard the screams,' he said. 'They ran out into the lift hall in a great panic. What did you do? Bite their legs?'

He led the way up the avenue and around the back of it, where a little lane led to the High Street of Merton Major.

They caught the bus back home, but this time Reggie had to sit under the stairs as all the seats were taken. He sprawled out and tried to sleep, but the bus, going over some badly rutted road, bounced viciously, and he banged his chin on the floor. He decided to sit up instead, leaning against the wall, and there he stayed until they reached Merton Minor, the regulars remarking on how well Waldorf had behaved and how well trained he was.

Jim was still considered a bit of an oddity by a lot of local people who stopped to talk to him as they got off the bus, and stroked Reggie's ears and asked how Mr Bagshott-Hawkes was progressing. Jim fended them off with the standard comment, 'as well as can be expected,' and as usual everyone appeared satisfied with the answer, as they really expected nothing else. Jim and Reggie left them talking amongst themselves, and heard fragments of conversation such as, 'nervous breakdown', 'working too hard' and 'always affects the quiet ones the worst'.

Lucy let them in when they got back to The Elms and the house smelled of cooking. The big kitchen table was covered with plates of sandwiches and freshly baked tarts and cakes.

'It's the WI meeting tonight,' said Lucy in answer to Jim's enquiring look. 'Once a month in the village hall and we always get a lot there. Did you see Reggie? I phoned through and said that I didn't know whether or not you would be going. There's still no change in him. I'm between two stools. I want to go and I dread going. Can you understand that?' She looked away and wiped her hands on the tea towel. Reggie walked across and rubbed himself against her legs. It was breaking him up to see Lucy like this, but he consoled himself that, with any luck, it wouldn't be for long now.

'Please God,' he thought to himself, 'don't let anything go wrong.' Desperately he rubbed his head against Lucy, nearly knocking her over in his emotion.

'Ah, Waldorf, Waldorf,' she said, stooping down and hugging him tightly to her. 'D'you see, Mr Contrell, he knows there's something wrong, don't you boy?'

'He sure does, ma'am,' said Jim, afraid to catch Reggie's eye. 'Sometimes these animals have a lot more intelligence than they're given credit for.' He turned away, saying 'Good night, see you tomorrow,' and walked to the door where he stopped and turned. 'You never know,' he added, 'but a couple more days might make all the difference to Reggie.' With this he turned on his heel and went out into the night.

Chapter Eleven

Reggie awoke with a start, the violence of his dream forcing him awake. His heart was pounding and every hair on his back was standing straight up. It took him some minutes to realise who or what he was. He clambered to his feet, all four of them, and the nightmare of his situation came back to him forcefully. Despair gripped him physically as he stumbled to the conservatory windows and looked out.

It was just after six and a grey dawn was breaking. Scuds of rain were still gusting across while the fir trees which formed a compact hedge at the sides of the garden were being whipped and rippled as waves created by the wind ran along them. The wind was beginning to scream around the conservatory in a manner that he hadn't experienced before. The word 'hurricane' clicked up in his mind and he pushed it out again immediately. There had been nothing on the box last night about a hurricane, only a forecast of very strong winds and bursts of rain. Clouds of leaves, like large dark snow flakes, filled the air to such an extent that it seemed a wonder to him that there would be any left on the trees.

He shivered, and felt the need for action. He ran to the back door and, after turning the large key with his teeth, opened it and ran out into the drive. Turning right at the entrance, he ran furiously on up to High Tor as if all the devils in the world were after him. Sometimes the wind blew him bodily over. Branches and twigs flew through the air along with the leaves and the wind was becoming so strong that he had a job to catch his breath. When he finally reached High Tor, he had to go over the rim and lie down in the lee to regain it.

He didn't rest there long. He got up and made his way through the ferns and brambles that now looked like a dark green sea, swirling and seething as fierce gusts swept across them. Arriving at the slit in the bank that they had earmarked as their sanctuary, he looked out across the large depression and his heart sank even further. If this weather kept up, would the spaceship be able to land, and how about getting Waldorf out of the hospital and up here?

God! The thought struck him. He'd have to get back. No more trouble, please! Why hadn't he stopped to think? If Lucy got up and found him missing, all hell would break loose again. He started to run, battling against the wind and rain, and was panting like mad when he finally arrived home and let himself in, locked the door and made his way to his basket in the conservatory.

He'd hardly had the time to settle down when he saw Lucy coming into the kitchen in her dressing-gown. She let out a startled scream when she saw him.

'You're all wet, Waldorf,' she cried. 'You've been out, haven't you?' She went to the back door and tried the lock and the next minute she was on the phone to Gus, having a job to make herself understood through all the crackling and buzzing that was coming over the line.

Gus was there within minutes, his overcoat soaking wet. He looked at the still wet paw marks in the kitchen by the back door and examined Reggie's drenched coat and dirty paws. He stood up and scratched his head, completely at a loss, then walked back to the back door and examined it.

'This key is wet,' he said.

'Yes,' said Lucy. 'It was when I looked at it.' Gus took a pencil out of his pocket and, slipping it through the hole at the end of the key, he unlocked the door and took the key out.

'Have you got an envelope that I could put this in?' he asked. When one was produced, he carefully put the key into it and sealed the flap, wrote upon it 'Key to Bagshott-Hawkes' house' and put it in his pocket.

'I'm going to give this to the lab boys to see

what they can make of it. I think I'd better ask the chief if one of the policewomen can stay with you for a couple of days and nights until we can get to the bottom of what's going on here.' He went and sat down at the dining-room table to write out his report. When he had finished, he read it over to Lucy, going back to the beginning of his notes, starting when Reggie and Waldorf had first vanished.

'All this is connected, it's obvious,' he said. 'I wish he could talk.' He nodded his head towards Reggie, who was listening to all that was going on and cursing himself for being so brainless as to have caused this new upheaval. Not like his normal self at all.

Gus was speaking again. 'Now it stands to reason that, if that back door was locked and the front door is still locked and bolted, then whoever let the dog out and then back in must still be in here.'

All the colour drained from Lucy's face and she swayed slightly.

'Now sit down, Lucy,' said Gus firmly, 'while I get on the phone and call someone up here to help us search the place.'

He gave up on the phone after a couple of minutes and went out to his van to use the radio. Half an hour later a constable and a policewoman arrived, looking wet and wind-blown, and were let in through the front door.

'Took your time getting here,' said Gus to the young constable with some asperity.

'It's the weather, Sarge,' said Robert, the young constable. 'It's a wonder that we made it at all what with a couple of trees being blown down across the road.'

'Well, never mind that now,' said Gus. 'We have reason to believe that we have an intruder in the house, so I want this place searched thoroughly. And watch your back, we've got no idea of who or what we're looking for.'

The search was painstaking. Nothing was missed. Reggie, lying on the floor, watched them, giving a half-hearted wag of the tail as a form of apology whenever anybody came near him during the search. Finally they all gathered together in the kitchen, drinking coffee and trying to untangle the puzzle.

'Jenny, I want you to stay here with Mrs Bagshott-Hawkes,' said Gus, 'that is until I can get someone to relieve you. Too many odd things have happened in this house in the last couple of days when Mrs Bagshott-Hawkes hasn't been around.' He stopped. A look of enlightenment crossed his face. 'As a matter of fact,' and here he paused. 'As a matter of fact,' he went on, 'the only one present every time was Waldorf.' Everybody stopped drinking their coffee and turned to stare accusingly at Reggie, who tried to look innocent and thumped Waldorf's tail up and down feeling as guilty as hell.

The room went quiet as they all now turned their attention to Gus who was standing there with his cup of coffee in his hand, staring into space.

'I've been thinking,' said Gus slowly. 'Supposing it's Waldorf that is the attraction? What if we get rid of him? I don't mean having him put down or anything like that' – pure terror gripped Reggie and his bowels threatened an immediate evacuation – 'I mean have him locked up somewhere safe so that if he *is* the reason that someone is getting in here they won't find him. I'm not saying that anyone *is* getting in here, mind,' he added hastily, 'but there might be some psychic force – not that I believe in any such nonsense,' he added, 'but you never know, and what with what's happened to Mr Bagshott-Hawkes . . . Which hasn't been explained as yet, well . . . you don't know do you?' He floundered and stopped, taking a hasty swig of his coffee.

Reggie was appalled. His stomach made a mad gurgling noise and his muscles contracted at the thought that he may be forced to miss the rendezvous. He cursed his stupid impetuosity at losing control of himself and causing all this havoc.

Lucy was speaking. 'Well, I think that's all right, Gus, but where will you take him?'

'We'll take him down to the police station where we can keep an eye on him for a few days and see if these occurrences stop. He'll be OK there. Be spoiled rotten, I should think. Take him for walks. They'll probably think he's a police dog. Might do his image a bit of good.' He cast a sardonic glance in Reggie's direction.

'Oh, I think that that will be fine then,' said Lucy. 'Mr Contrell's been taking him out for walks. He's very good with him. I've never seen Waldorf get on with anybody so well as he gets on with him, except Reggie of course.'

'That's OK,' said Gus. 'Tell him that if he wants to take Waldorf out for a walk to come down to the station and pick him up. Meanwhile, Jenny here will stay with you and keep you company. Where's your friend? Dulcie, isn't it? Be a good idea to have her here at night to keep you company as well. The more the merrier, I say. Now where's his lead? He won't mind travelling in the van, will he? Here you are, Robert.' This to the young constable. 'Take him with you and put him in one of the cells till I get in. I'm going home to finish my breakfast and change into my uniform. Now cut along there a bit sharpish. They'll be queuing up at the station by now I shouldn't wonder.' He turned and winked at Lucy.

Reggie was aghast. Put him in one of the cells? He sat up, gazing at them in what he thought was a pleading manner, but it looked to the four people standing around him more like the start of a fit, and they all stepped back apprehensively.

'Come on, Robert,' said Gus. 'Stop messing around and get hold of him.'

'Half a minute, Sarge,' said Robert, 'I don't think that's a very good idea at the moment. There's all hell broken loose at the station over this hurricane. We've got practically every road closed and some of the ambulances can't get through.'

'What do you mean, hurricane and ambulances can't get through? What are you talking about?'

'People hit by slates and flying glass and whatever. The hospitals are chocker, we've even got people sleeping in the cells.'

'Why the devil didn't they call me?' asked Gus.

'I thought they had,' said Robert, 'but there must have been a cock-up somewhere.' Lucy stepped forward. 'Come on, Waldorf,' she coaxed, 'there's a good boy.' Reggie went up to her crying and howling while she stroked his head. He kept on trying to tell her that he didn't want to go to the police station, especially now that he was so near to getting back to normal, but Lucy had been persuaded, and once her mind had been made up it took a lot of changing.

Abruptly he shut up. It was no use whining on. He'd go along with it and make his escape on the way to the station. But once again he was frustrated. Gus was speaking.

'On second thoughts, and seeing how the weather is playing up, it may be better to phone your kennels – you do put him in the kennels now and again, don't you? Have them look after him for a while until we can get this little lot sorted out.'

Reggie howled. He sat back on his haunches, put back his head and really howled. It was a terrible noise. He started charging about the room looking for a way out, but all the doors were shut and he didn't feel brave enough to jump through the window as he had seen some dogs do on television. In any case, if he jumped through the window he would probably be blown straight back in again, such was the force of the wind. Finally he shut up, more through frustration than common sense, and backed under the dining table, quite prepared to defend himself with his large Waldorf teeth if they tried to catch hold of him. Surprisingly, they left him there.

It was half past two before the man from the kennels arrived, moaning about having to make a detour of several miles because of fallen trees and some flooding. He was in a bad temper and soaking wet to boot. Reggie looked at him without recognition.

This was not the usual man form the kennels and Reggie was revolted at the sight of him. The painfully thin young man, dressed in a uniform that was much too big for him, was pimply and full of the sense of his own importance. He advanced upon Reggie who was still ensconced under the table.

'What's 'is name?' the slightly nasal voice enquired.

'Waldorf,' said Lucy, 'and he's normally such a stupid old thing, but he's lost his master and he isn't taking it very well.'

'Waldorf? That's a funny name for a dog. Gor, 'e's a big 'un. Come on, boy.'

Reggie backed away as far as he could go, which was not very far as he came up against the radiator which was so hot that it burned his backside and he shuffled forward again.

'I'll 'ave to get the noose for this 'un,' said Pimples. 'Shan't be a tick.' And he was gone, bounding out of the house into the rain that was now lashing down in a fury. He soon returned, soaked, carrying a metal pole as long as a broom handle that had a thin rope noose at one end that could be pulled tight.

'Now this won't hurt 'im,' said Pimples jovially. ''E'll kick up a bit of a racket and pull me all over the place at first, so I'd like one of yous to give me 'an 'and when I got the rope over 'im.' He looked pointedly at the young policewoman.

Reggie gazed imploringly at Lucy and howled pitifully. It would have been better for him if he had just lain down and let things happen, but he was new to being a dog and his knowledge of what was going to happen overrode his human common sense. The chairs were pulled away from the dining-room table and Pimples advanced with the pole held out in front of him, the loop of rope hanging from it. Reggie backed away, showing Waldorf's teeth, but when his rear end touched the boiling radiator again he gave a yelp and lunged forward, obligingly putting his head straight through the loop which was immediately pulled tight, not tight enough to strangle him, but let it be said that it wasn't very comfortable.

He shook his head, trying to get free, but the loop was now fixed and all that Pimples and Jenny had to do was hold the pole tight and he was helpless. He came to his human senses then and gave up immediately. He was led, unprotesting, by the pole, to the van parked in the drive.

The van was one of those specials, its side windows covered with wire mesh so that they could be opened without fear of the passengers absconding. Reggie stared miserably through the back at Lucy until she went out of his vision as the van turned a bend in the road, and then he took stock of his situation. His confidence that he would be able to extricate himself from this mess took a nose dive. The only way that he was going to get out of the van was if somebody let him out. His paws were too big to go through the mesh, which was unfortunate as he could quite easily have lifted out the staple which fastened it in place if he could have reached it. But first he would have to remove the loop from around his neck and that was going to be difficult, as Pimples seemed to be labouring under the delusion that he was a rally driver, and the gusting wind wasn't a great help. Reggie was sliding from one side of the van to the other and at one point the loop threatened to strangle him when one of his involuntary rolls caused the end of the pole to jam in a corner and he was held by the neck until the centrifugal force diminished as the van was straightened up before hurtling around another bend.

On one of the straight bits, he managed to hook a paw through the loop and pull it over his head and off. He was now able to lie on the floor almost flat, with his legs spread out to stabilise himself and conceal the noose under his body. The journey didn't take long. When they halted in the yard of the kennels, Pimples came around to the back of the van and opened the doors, quite unconcerned, confident that he had only to grab the pole which he had left quite handy and he would be in complete charge of this large grey monster.

Rude awakenings can be quite amusing to watch, but Reggie had neither the time nor the inclination to stay and witness Pimples' discomfiture when, as he was reaching, albeit carefully, for the pole, Reggie leapt to his feet and sprang over his outstretched arm. Landing on the ground, he turned sharply and bolted through the gate which was being closed by another of the kennel staff, who immediately gave chase. But it was a hopeless task as the kennels were on a lane in the open country near to Merton Minor, and it took but a moment for Reggie to slip through the ditch at the side of the road, on through a gap in the hedge and over an unkempt field of scrub grass and brambles. After turning and twisting a dozen times he threw his pursuers off the scent and found himself on the edge of a golf course. He lay down under a hedge to get his breath back and looked back the way he had come to see if anybody was coming after him.

There was nobody and he gave a relieved grin to himself. It came out as a sort of twisted snarl that would have frightened anyone had they been near enough to see it.

He rested there for some time, secure in the knowledge that he had lost them, but on looking around he realised that he had only a vague idea of where he was. He knew of the golf course, but had never been here before. It was an old-fashioned club that didn't have lady members and because of that, Lucy and her friends had boycotted it in their social rounds.

He had driven past it many times in his human life and knew that if he could get to the road, he would probably be able to find his way to . . . That was a thought, where could he go? No good going home – that would be the first place they'd look for him. But he had to go somewhere; he was so starving that he even thought of those glutinous Meaty Chunks with longing. His best bet would be to make his way to Jim's house. At least he would be sure of a welcome there – he hoped. No good trying to sneak home and raid the fridge, they would make sure every key was safely put away from now on.

He started to think about Sunday. Two days to go. He had to get back. Without him, Reggie, the exchange couldn't take place, and if he didn't show up before it was time for Jim to snatch Waldorf out of the hospital, Jim wouldn't have any reason to risk it. It would be no good his kidnapping Waldorf on the off chance that Reggie might show up.

Reggie found that he was running like a mad thing over the top of the golf course, and forced himself to slow down and think. He mustn't be spotted at the side of town where both he and Jim lived. People must be led to think that he had made his escape the other way. He sat down on his haunches and thought about it. He would have to hide away somewhere until it was fairly dark. It was a good five miles to Jim's house by the round-about route he would have to take, so if he started out just before dark his natural grey colour would melt into the background and he had a good chance of arriving without being seen. He went into a copse of trees, a natural hazard, and looked for shelter from the driving rain. There was none.

The weather was still wild and the trees were swaying, branches crashing against each other in a frightening manner. He ran out of the copse and on down across the golf course to the entrance where in a lean-to shed at the back he saw about six of the greens staff sitting on a bench, drinking tea or coffee out of flasks and eating sandwiches.

'Gor, look at 'im!' said one of them. 'Like a drowned rat. Come on, boy.' He broke off a piece of sandwich and tossed it towards Reggie who sniffed at it suspiciously before wolfing it down. Ham sandwich with a hint of mustard. No hesitation with the next piece that was tossed towards him. Woof. Gone. Several more pieces of various sandwiches and cake were thrown over and went the same way. Emboldened, he walked over to them and lay down.

'Wonder where he's come from?' said another of them. 'They say that this weather isn't fit for a dog, and judging by him, they're right.' He reached over and rubbed Reggie's ears.

'Well, I think we'll call it a day,' said another of them who appeared to be the boss. 'We're not going to get sod all done in this.'

'What about 'im?' asked the man who had tossed the first piece of sandwich.

'Leave him where he is,' said the boss man, 'he'll make his way back home, I expect, when this weather improves. He can't do any harm here, and if we scooted him out, he'd probably come back in when we've gone.' A couple of them threw their remaining sandwiches and cakes down for him and five minutes later he was on his own. It seemed an age before the leaden sky began to darken further and he left his refuge and started off.

He settled into a steady lope and when he reached the road he waited in the hedge until he was sure it was clear before he crossed, trusting to his sense of direction that he was going the right way. He must have misjudged it somehow as, once it was properly dark, he realised he was lost. He tried to find some high ground so that he could get his bearings, but the darkness defeated him. Looking at the sky from where he was, he could see three areas of cloud where the orange light of the sodium lamps was reflected, but which belonged to Merton Minor he had no idea. If he could have seen the stars, he would have had a good idea of which was which, but in this cold, wet, overcast darkness he gave up.

'Waldorf would have had no such difficulty,' he thought bitterly. 'He would have just switched on his inbuilt radar system or whatever it was that acted as a direction finder, put his nose in the direction that it indicated and followed it right to where he wanted to go.'

His stomach rumbled. He had never felt so hungry in his life. Or so wet. Or so cold. Or so miserable. He got to his feet and padded on slowly and carefully. Was he going the right way? He didn't know. Was that car that had just gone past going to or coming from Merton Minor? He cursed his height. Those extra three feet that he had been used to in his old body had given him an advantage that he hadn't appreciated. If he had his old body he would be able to see over that damned hedge, but there, if he had his old body, he wouldn't be in this predicament. He trotted along, following the direction that the car had taken, towards one of the orange patches in the sky, its dim light reflecting off the wet road just enough to let him see where he was going.

The rain had become a drizzle and thank God the wind had started to abate. The water ran off him as if he had been thrown into a river. He stopped to rest his weary paws. The brook in the ditch behind him was almost full, a rushing torrent after all the rain there had been of late, and he went over to get a drink to help quell the hunger pains that were racking his stomach. He heard a bus whining towards him and read the sign on the front of it as it went by. 'Swiffield via Tetlebury'. The bus roared on and its tail lights were soon lost to view as it went around a bend in the road. Reggie sat down to think. That bus had come from Merton Major, so he was going the right way for Merton Minor. His heart lifted and he trotted off in the gloom towards familiar territory.

It took him two hours to reach the main road and another half an hour to reach the turn-off for Merton Minor, because he had to keep stopping and hiding in the long grass at the side of the road when traffic went by. Eventually he arrived at Main Street and, stopping every now and then to avoid the odd pedestrian, he finally arrived at Jim's house. He heard a noise at the rear of the side path and saw that it was Mrs Contrell, Jim's mother, putting some rubbish in the bin. Standing on his hind legs at the gate, he gave a soft bark and rattled the gate at the same time. Mrs Contrell, who was about to enter the back door of her cottage, turned with a start.

'Who's there?' she called. Reggie gave another bark, of welcome he hoped, and shook the gate again. Mrs Contrell walked back slowly and cautiously to the back gate and suddenly realised that the great beast shaking the gate was Waldorf, or so she supposed.

'Is that you, Waldorf?' she called.

Another shake of the gate and a short bark of affirmation. She came to the gate and opened it to let him in.

'I suppose you're looking for Jim,' she said. 'Well, he's gone looking for you, so you must have passed each other somehow.' She took a tin of small cakes from the larder and, taking two out, broke them up and gave them to him. They were gone in a flash and he cursed himself for his apparent lack of manners, but he hadn't come up with any other way of eating with the dental set-up inherited from Waldorf.

'My, you're hungry,' she exclaimed, watching the rapid disappearance of the cakes. 'I'd rather keep you a week than a fortnight, as the saying goes. Where have you been anyhow, my boy? Running off like that. Your poor old missus has enough to put up with, without you acting up.' She fondled his ears and he moaned with pleasure. She went on, 'The whole world seems to have gone crazy at the moment, though I can't complain. Having Jim back normal is as marvellous for us as your poor old master going off his head is bad for your missus. Seems that that's the way of life, giving and taking, but the sense of it all escapes me.'

She got out of the old rocking chair in which she had seated herself, and made her way into the passage. He lumbered to his feet and followed her down the hall to a phone that was secured to the wall. Realising her intention, he sat back on his haunches and howled. Mrs Contrell jumped.

'What on earth is the matter with you?' she asked, stroking his ears. Reggie nuzzled her hand.

'There's a good old boy,' said Mrs Contrell, puzzled by this show of affection. Reggie continued nuzzling her hand, his brain racing. He had to stop her from getting to the phone and ringing Lucy, because it was as clear as a bell to him that that had been her plan. He tried to remember how the dog heroes he had occasionally seen on the box got away with things and manipulated human beings to do what they wanted.

He walked away from Mrs Contrell, giving a little moan and looking back over his shoulder. She looked after him nonplussed. He gave another little moan and jerked his head in an invitation to follow, not, he realised too late, in a doggy way, but in a human way. He must have done it right, though, because she responded to his gesture immediately, and followed him into the warmth of the kitchen where he gave another twitch of his head and she sat in the rocker again and fondled his ears.

'What is the matter with you?' she asked again in some exasperation. 'Now you wait here. I'm going to phone your missus.' She went to get up out of the chair.

Reggie flopped on his back in front of her feet with his legs in the air, preventing her from getting up out of the chair in the same way as he had seen Waldorf cajoling Lucy. But suddenly he realised that he was exposing his penis to her and he leapt up on to his feet with one paw clamped to himself in desperation, leaning against her and howling.

'You silly old thing! What is the matter with you? Now stop that noise, for goodness' sake. What's the matter with your stomach then? Here. Let me have a look.'

Using his weight he leaned more heavily against her, wishing with all his heart that he was wearing trousers. But if he was wearing trousers, where would he put his tail? He thought of cartoons on the telly, with drawings of ridiculous foxes wearing shorts with their tails sticking out of specially cut holes in the back. He stopped howling and changed his tack, turning his head to lick her hand.

'Daft as a brush, you are,' she said. 'We'd better wait until Jim comes home. He'll know what to do with you. It's like having another baby about the house.'

Relieved, Reggie lay down on his stomach on the warm rag mat.

'Thank goodness for that,' he thought. 'It'll be hard enough getting it over to Jim when he comes home.' He felt his eyes closing. This was luxury indeed.

Chapter Twelve

'He's there by the fire,' said Mrs Contrell when Jim finally walked in. 'Came in through the back gate about an hour ago and made an awful fuss at first, but he's been nice and quiet ever since.'

Reggie stood up as Jim entered the room.

'Hello, stupid,' said Jim, leaning over to give Reggie a pat and a pull of the ears. 'You've been at it again, haven't you? Not using your brains. I know all about it. I've been up at the house talking to your missus and she's in a fair old state. They're blaming your presence in the house as being some sort of magnet for a psychic visitation or something weird, and that was why they were putting you in the kennels. But of course you know that already. It's a pity that you don't use your brains a bit more, you know what I mean? Those Reggie-trained brains that you have up there.' Here tapping Reggie's head rather hard with his knuckle. 'It's your own fault, messing about like that. Now I'm going to get on the phone and tell them that you're here and ask them if you can stay for a couple of days. Mam!' This shouted over his shoulder at his mother. 'Have we got anything that we can feed him with? If not, I'll ask them now if I can pop down for some of his grub. I expect he's starving.'

'Goodness me, Jim, there's no need for you to shout like that. I'm only here, right behind you, and listening to you talking to that dog. If I didn't know that we two were the only ones here, I'd have thought that you were speaking to another person, not just a dog, although by the look of him he understands every word you say.'

'Oh, he understands all right, don't you, old son?' He addressed this to Reggie who let out a quick affirmative bark. Mrs Contrell gave a quick nod of her head.

'I really think that he does,' she said, advancing into the room to the grate where she pulled the kettle over the flames. 'Your brother will be back in a minute so I'm making a cup of tea. Do you want anything?'

'I'm just going to make this quick phone call and I'll be back with his grub in a couple of minutes, then I'll have some of that shepherd's pie with a mug of tea, if that's OK. Shan't be long.' He strode to the phone in the passage and was almost immediately connected.

Lucy sounded strained on the phone, he thought, and said that she was glad he had rung. She wanted to see him urgently because something strange had happened. He hurried to the door, pulling on his parka as he went, and bumped into his brother coming in from the pub. It was, 'Hi Len, Hi Jim,' as they passed each other and Len came on through to where his mother was waiting at the kitchen door.

'And where's old secretive off to at this time of night, Mam?' Len asked his mother, glancing back at the door.

'Gone to get some food for our new lodger,' said his mother, indicating through the kitchen door. Len went past her with enquiring eyes, and as he entered the kitchen, Reggie got up from the mat and slowly wagged his tail.

'Oh, it's you, is it, you false old sod?' said Len, reaching over and giving him a pat. 'And what further mayhem have you been up to? I hear that you've been a bad boy again.'

'What's he supposed to have done now?' asked Mrs Contrell. 'We know all about him running away from the kennels, if that's what you're talking about.'

'No, Mam,' said Len, 'this was earlier in the week. You know Myra Tait? Lives at the back of your friend Lucy's house. You know her, got that nasty little pug dog. Well this 'un here grabbed him by the scruff of the neck, by all accounts, and dunked him in that big water butt, you know, the one by Lucy's garage, and every time he came up screaming, old Waldorf, who wouldn't hurt a fly, pushed him back under again. He let him get out in the end, but they reckon Pug will never be the same again.'

'Serve him right, nasty little brute,' said Mrs Contrell, an amused smile playing around her lips. 'But somebody's having you on. He couldn't have done that.'

'Well, PG came into the pub tonight – you know PG. Lives at Wits End, the house next door to Reggie and Lucy. Well, he came in and said little Jason, you know, his son, saw the whole thing from his tree house. You know how he dotes on that boy. Tells us all the things that he gets up to. He's even put a photo of him behind the bar. We all laughed at him, of course; we all know the tall yarns he tells, but old Stan Tait was there and said that Pug had come home soaked, with bloody marks on his neck, and they'd had to get the vet. Myra went storming off to Lucy's house when she saw the trail of water coming from there, but there was nobody in except Waldorf and he was locked in. Then PG said, "Yes. That's quite right, Waldorf locked himself in," and the whole pub exploded with laughter. Myra left a note there for Lucy to phone her, according to old Stan, and when Lucy phoned and she went back there and showed Lucy what had happened, Lucy decided to get the police.'

Reggie had listened to this with growing horror. He was still lying down, but his tail stopped wagging and his stomach gave a series of moans and gurgles, various sphincter muscles opening and closing as panic started to grip him. Two pairs of eyes swivelled around to him.

'Gosh! He must be really hungry,' said Mrs Contrell. 'Did you hear that?' Len nodded speculatively. 'There's something odd about you, mister,' he said slowly and accusingly to Reggie. 'You and that bugger that's just gone out.'

'I wish you'd watch your language, Len, it's not very nice,' said Mrs Contrell, clicking her tongue in disapproval. 'Talking about your brother like that.'

'Well it's true,' said Len. 'If you think about it, the first two days that we had Jim back here as normal were great. Of course we had to get used to him being normal, but that's what I mean. We knew he was normal, but . . . I don't know . . . he seemed to alter all of a sudden. Something in the back of his mind that he's not telling us; and that damned dog's mixed up in it somehow.' He stared directly at Reggie who looked guiltily away. Len went on, 'And Jason said some other things about him,' nodding again at Reggie, 'that were odd. 'Course, when PG told us about him, we all laughed and took it for another of his tall ones; turning on the hose pipe and washing down the yard, unlocking the door with his teeth, and goodness knows what else.' He sat back in his chair and sipped the tea that his mother had put there for him.

'I think that's a bit far-fetched, if you ask me,' said Mrs Contrell. Len just grunted and resolved to keep an eye on the pair of them from now on.

Reggie squirmed with dismay. It was all he could

do to stop himself from rushing to the door and howling to be let out so that he could go after Jim. Gradually the panic subsided and he lay there, still tense. He hoped that if he acted like a normal dog, perhaps all Len's suspicions would go away.

Meanwhile Jim walked down the road towards The Elms, whistling to himself as he went. At least some of the pieces of the jigsaw were beginning to fall into place. What with the hurricane striking and Reggie being sent to the kennels it had looked as if the whole scheme was going to unravel before it had even got started. He wondered what it was that Lucy had wanted to see him about so urgently. Nothing untoward had happened as far as he was aware.

By now the wind had dropped considerably and the rain had stopped. There were a lot of muddy tracks on the lane where tractors had been running back and forth, cutting up and removing the few trees that had fallen across it and making safe those that had been damaged and left in a precarious condition. He had heard reports of three thousand trees being blown down in the south of England and of over a dozen people being killed. Sevenoaks in Kent had lost six of its oak trees, and would probably be known as One Oak from now on, he mused with a wry grin.

The hospitals had been inundated with casualties. Cuts from broken glass and flying slates, broken bones, heart attacks and premature births; the whole range of emergencies had stretched the resources of every hospital in the southern counties.

'It may,' he thought, 'be a good thing in the end for me and Reggie. It's an ill wind . . .' With all the hustle and bustle and weary staff, there would be a better chance for him to pull off the scheme that was hatching in his head.

At Reggie's house Lucy answered the door, worry lines etched on her face, and motioned him inside. He found Dulcie Nicholas standing behind her but she looked more puzzled than worried.

'Evening, Mrs B-H,' he said, trying to put a bright and breezy timbre in his voice.

'Evening, Jim,' said Lucy. 'You'd better come on through, there are a couple of people here who want to meet you, and talk to you about Waldorf.'

'Waldorf?' said Jim. 'Has he done something else? Killed a sheep or something?' He saw that there was a young policewoman there as well as Gus Mcleod.

'This is WPC Bentham and of course you know Gus,' said Lucy. 'And you probably know the lady and gentleman over there, Mr and Mrs Tait.'

Jim nodded his head in acknowledgement and murmured a quiet, 'Good evening.'

Seeing Jim's obvious ignorance of what was going on, Dulcie volunteered, 'We've had some information as to an incident here last Monday.' A mischievous smile played around her lips for a second and was suppressed with an obvious effort. 'Better let Gus fill you in. He knows more about it than I do.' She had a job to stop giggling.

'It's like this, Mr Contrell,' said Gus, picking up his notebook that was lying on the table. 'Last Monday . . .' and he went on to relate Pug's traumatic experience.

'Now we have had a witness come forward to say that he saw Waldorf pick up Pug by the neck and dunk him in the water butt which was full to the brim at the time but was four inches down after the attack, as Mrs Bagshott-Hawkes and Mrs Nicholas can vouch. What's more, the bloody marks on Pug's neck were, according to the vet, caused by the teeth of a large dog.

'Another thing, this same witness maintains that—' He stopped, plainly embarrassed, and snapped his notebook shut. 'Well, some other things seem to have happened on a previous occasion but we won't go into that now.'

Jim stared at him with what he hoped was a look of utter disbelief and then turned and looked slowly around at the others. Only Dulcie's face showed that she thought she had been listening to a load of old codswallop. Everybody else was serious. Jim took a deep breath.

'You're joking, of course,' he said lightly. (He would kill Reggie when he got hold of him.)

'No, sir,' said Gus.

'You mean to tell me that you believe this nonsense?' said Jim, deliberately showing that he was trying to keep a straight face.

'What I believe is irrelevant, sir,' said Gus. 'Mrs Tait made a complaint about a dangerous dog, and I must investigate the complaint, as you are probably well aware, sir.'

'Granted,' said Jim. 'But I've never heard anything like it. Who's this witness anyhow? Must have been drunk. If Waldorf was as clever as that, he'd be worth a fortune to his owner. All the world's circuses would be after him. Have you seen him? A sloth has more go than him. He's up at the cottage now, fasto in front of the fire; all he moves for is his food. By the way, Mrs B-H, have you got that food for him?'

Dulcie stood up. 'I'll get it,' she said, and disappeared into the kitchen, returning almost immediately with a supermarket bag in which could be seen the outlines of tins of Meaty Chunks and a large bag of biscuits.

'I know that Waldorf is staying with you, sir,' said Gus. 'Now mind that you look after him and keep him safe. We may have to have him examined.'

'Don't worry, Sergeant. If I have to take him out, he'll be on a lead, I assure you, and when he's at home he'll be kept in. I'd better get going, as it's getting late and I've got a pretty full day tomorrow.' He got to his feet, saying, 'Goodnight all, and don't worry, I'll take good care of Wal.'

There was a shout from Mrs Tait. 'Hang on a minute.' She glowered at Gus Mcleod. 'Aren't you going to do something? You can't let it go like that. That dog's dangerous. Can't you arrest it or something? Lock it up?' She was red with anger.

Gus Mcleod looked at her.

'Now, Mrs Tait,' he said quietly, 'you know that we've only got the one witness, and you know who it is. Let's look at this from what would be a normal point of view. Imagine the headlines. Now I know that you have made a serious complaint and I know that your dog was attacked and almost drowned . . . But look at the explanation we are going to have to give. We'd be laughed out of court. You know what they're going to say about our witness. Too active an imagination. If we had another witness, or if Waldorf had a history of bad behaviour, we'd have something to go to court with, but he is normally . . . well . . . a slightly animated hearth rug. I'm sorry, Mrs Bagshott-Hawkes, but that's how he is. He would be fast asleep in the well of the court and people could walk all over him and he wouldn't budge. The only one that could ever get him going was Reggie, and by the way, if it ever did go to court they could say that perhaps Waldorf was emotionally upset because he was missing Reggie, who is seriously ill in hospital, and what with our witness's story . . . Let's leave it for the weekend, Mrs Tait, and we'll look at it again on Monday.'

'But—' said Mrs Tait, now on her feet, but her husband Stan put his hand on her arm and motioned for her to stop.

'It makes sense, Myra,' he said. 'It makes a damned sight more sense than that other story. Now come on, love, leave it till Monday, like Mr Mcleod has suggested. It's getting late, as Jim says, so let's stop it here and all go home and get a good night's sleep.' He stood up and took his wife's arm.

'I'm not very happy about this,' she said, 'but I do see what you mean.' She glared at Jim. 'You'd better look after that dog,' she said with venom in her voice. 'He's going to kill somebody someday, and then, perhaps, we'll get some justice done.' She pulled her coat tightly around her and headed for the door and out without so much as a goodnight. Poor old Stan, looking apologetic, floundered after her.

An uncomfortable silence descended on the room.

'I'd better be going,' said Jim awkwardly, and made his way towards the door. He wished that he could comfort Lucy and reassure her that everything would come out all right, but he couldn't. If the story about Waldorf that they had just heard sounded a little bit off-centre, what would the truth about him and Reggie sound like?

Dulcie came to the door with him and he turned to her to say goodnight.

'Well,' she said, 'you can't say that nothing ever happens in Merton. Goodnight, Jim. Tell Waldorf to make sure that everything is locked up safe and secure tonight.' He heard her laughing as she shut the door behind him.

He hurried up the lane to the cottage. Len and his mother were still sitting in the kitchen, and they both looked up as he walked in. They could see in his face that something was wrong. Reggie was on his feet, looking at him as well, wanting to get him on his own so that he could attempt to tell Jim what he had heard, if that were at all possible.

'You've been a long time, son,' said his mother.

'Yeah,' said Len, 'we've been waiting for you to come back. I heard some funny stories about him—' indicating Reggie who sat back on his haunches in dismay. 'That PG was down at the pub tonight, swears that what he was telling us was true, any rate, swears that what Jason told him was true.'

'Come and sit down, Jim, and, I'll get your supper out of the oven. There's tea in the pot, and more hot water in the kettle. We can talk when you're eating.'

Jim came back from hanging up his coat in the passage and sat at the table. He couldn't look at Reggie. Reggie could sense the anger boiling up in Jim, and his stomach gave its familiar whine.

'Hark at him,' said Mrs Contrell, 'he's starving. I'll go and open one of those tins and give him some biscuits as well.' She took a tin and the biscuits out of the bag and went over to the sink where the tin opener was screwed to the wall over the draining board. Reggie didn't move. The top came off the tin and the smell of succulent Meaty Chunks joined that of the shepherd's pie. There was a rattle as the dry biscuits clattered into the old tin plate and the meat was spooned over the top, and still Reggie didn't move.

Len, lying back in the rocker with another mug of tea in his hand, wagged a finger. 'There you are, see,' he said to no one in particular, 'that dog's not normal. If he was normal, he'd have been off the mat and over to his grub by now, 'cos if I can smell it, he can. Unless he's lost his sense of smell as well.'

Jim looked at him.

'What's the story about Waldorf?' he asked, knowing full well that it was going to be the one he had just heard.

Len proceeded to tell the tale and Jim let him go on, just in case there was something else to come out that hadn't been said at Lucy's house. Reggie cringed and crawled on his stomach under the table, completely ignoring the food that had been put down for him. Len came to the end of his recital and the silence was broken only by the hissing of a log on the fire and the singing of the kettle on the hob.

Finally Jim spoke.

'I've just come from Lucy's. The police are there, and Mr and Mrs Tait, and I've been told the same story. So it was little Jason that started all this, was it?'

Len grunted. 'It was that sod that started it.' He gestured towards Reggie trying to hide under the table. 'And you're mixed up in it somehow, and it's no good looking at me like that, I'm damned certain that you know what's going on.'

Jim looked at him. 'Come on, Len. Use your loaf. That kid must have a good imagination, that's all I can say. How old is he? Six? Seven? He's been watching too much TV. For God's sake use your eyes. Look at him. Come here, boy.' Poor old Reggie whined and crawled out from under the table, putting his paw on Jim's knee in supplication. He painted and let his tongue hang loose in the best Waldorf manner he could manage. Jim squeezed his ears hard and Reggie yelped.

'Get down and eat your food,' snapped Jim, and the tone in his voice brooked no opposition. Reggie dutifully went across to his food and saw off the noxious heap on the plate.

Len looked on morosely.

'There you are,' he said, 'look at that. He's not even your damned dog and here we are, just a couple of days since the pair of you had that rumpus in the pub, and he's doing exactly as you tell him. Not normal, not normal at all.'

Another long silence followed and Reggie became increasingly aware that he had an urgent need to go to the toilet. He went and stood by the door and gave a little whine. The two men watched him.

'He wants to go out,' said Len.

'Right,' said Jim, getting to his feet and opening the door. Reggie trotted to the back door and gave another little whine.

'OK,' said Jim, 'and don't be long. We've got a lot to do tomorrow.' Reggie slunk out and Jim shut the door after him then returned to the kitchen.

Chapter Thirteen

Saturday dawned sharp and crisp. A sudden unexpected frost had transformed all around into fairyland. Jim had risen early and looked in on Reggie whom he found gazing out of the window at the frosty landscape. Here, just on the edge of where the hurricane had scythed through, there was not all that much damage. The power was still on in the area even if the lights had flickered a few times when the winds were at their height. Jim switched on the radio news and heard harrowing tales of woe. A quarter of a million homes still without electricity.

Reggie gave a growl of greeting that he managed to make sound welcoming.

'Would you like some tea or coffee, Reggie?' asked Jim suddenly. It had just occurred to him that Reggie, used to civilised drinks, hadn't been offered one for the past week.

Reggie nodded his head vigorously.

'Nod your head. Tea?' a pause, 'or coffee . . . ? Right. Now, do you want your coffee black?' another pause, 'or white? OK. Sugar . . . one or two?' Reggie gave two short barks.

Jim made a large black coffee and after adding sugar, poured it into a basin and put it on the floor near Reggie, who gave a quick lap at the inviting brew and jumped back, yelping with pain. It was probably the same pain that a human tongue would have felt if it had been stuck into a hot cup of coffee, but his tongue was bigger. Quickly he lapped at his dish of water to cool it off. Fortunately he hadn't put it right in so he had only burned the tip. Jim watched him with mixed feelings of amusement and consternation. No, he thought, it was no good giving Reggie anything except recognised dog food. His dental arrangements were made for tearing meat and wolfing it down and as for drinking . . . well, lapping that was the order of the day. Besides, tomorrow should be the last day that he'd have to worry about Reggie's diet, if things went right.

He'd fixed on Sunday morning as the best time for the kidnap. Then there'd only be a few hours' wait for the rendezvous. He wished that he could have rehearsed what he would have to do tomorrow, so that everything would fall into place and run like a well-oiled clock, but that was impossible. He and Reggie must not be seen hanging around the hospital too much. After all, it wasn't as though Reggie could blend into the background. Not only was he a little large, but how many Irish wolfhounds were there roaming about, especially in hospitals? Not many. In fact, no dogs at all, except for guide dogs. In and out it would have to be, and a prayer that nothing would go wrong.

He went into the passage and shrugged on his warm parka, then made his way out to the back of the house and the lean-to shed where the tractor and horse box were kept. He clambered up into the tractor and started it up. He drove it in and out of the shed a few times, then put it back and switched it off. He checked the fuel; almost full. He went over to the horse box and checked that over. The four tyres on the close-coupled wheels were fully pumped up. He went around to the back and lowered the tailgate to look inside. There was a strong padded partition down the middle of the box so that two animals could be carried. Hanging up at the front were two hay nets so that the horses could have a snack as they went along, and rings were set in the side for tethering the two halters. He gave a last look around, then slung into the trailer a coil of rope that was hanging on a nail in the lean-to, closed the tailgate and made his way back into the welcome warmth of the cottage.

Both Len and his mother were up when he got in.

'What's with the tractor going at this time on a Saturday morning?' asked Len as he poured his mother and himself cups of tea out of the still hot teapot.

'Oh! I'm still fascinated by machinery,' said Jim, with as much conviction as he could manage. Len had that disbelieving look about him that had often appeared lately. In fact, Len was so used to being Jim's minder, and having to think for him, that he found most of Jim's actions surprising. Len went and sat in the old armchair in front of the fire, sipping his tea reflectively.

What was the bugger up to now, he thought to himself. He felt like a stranger to this Jim. Though he still looked pretty much the same as before, the change in his mental make-up had subtly altered other aspects of him as well. This new brother of his was one of the most self-assured people he had ever met. Not in a bombastic way, but with an air of quiet authority about him.

Reggie, sitting on the mat, could see the furrows of curiosity crossing Len's face and decided to do something to try to divert his thinking. Moving forward, he put his head on the man's knee. Len reached down and fondled Reggie's ears.

'And you, you false old sod. You've changed your tune since that night in the pub, haven't you? Think he's God now, but then . . . anyone would think that the devil hisself was after you. And what's he want that tractor for, first telling me that he's got a job on, and then he's "fascinated by machinery"? Pull the other one.' He sat there until his mother called, 'Breakfast on the table,' and giving Reggie a final pat, got up to join his family at the table.

* * *

Lucy was also up early on Saturday. At first light she had risen and gone downstairs, made a large pot of tea and taken a cup up to her friend.

'What on earth time is it, Lucy?' asked Dulcie, casting bleary eyes around. She was never at her best in the morning.

'Come on, Dulcie . . . it's only seven o'clock, I know, but I want us both to go and have a look round High Tor this morning. We should have thought of it at the beginning if we had used our heads. Come on. Put it all together. High Tor, Reggie, Waldorf and Jim Contrell. All linked. Reggie with brain damage, Jim Contrell with his brain cured and Waldorf! . . . He's different. Won't leave me alone. Followed me about as though he couldn't bear for me to be out of his sight. Look how he went mad when they took him to the kennels. It's not as though he hasn't been there before. He's been there heaps of times. They treat him just like one of the family when he's there. Matter of fact, the only times when he wasn't lying around sleeping were when Reggie took him out. So come on, put on something warm and a good pair of walking shoes. I'm going down to make us a big breakfast, and then we'll get the car out and see what we can find.' With that she turned and went down the stairs.

Dulcie turned over with a wail.

'Oh, come on Lucy. I was going to have my hair done this morning. Can't it wait till tomorrow?' She groaned when there was no reply. 'Besides, I've nothing here to wear for walking in the country.'

An hour later the two women, dressed for the weather, were driving up the lane past the Contrell cottage. Jim heard the car and, looking out of the window as it went past, recognised Lucy and Dulcie.

'Wonder what those two are up to?' he mused. He knew that there was nothing up there but farm gates leading into the fields and that at the top the lane petered out in a small clearing at the side of the bank leading up to High Tor.

The car reached the end of the lane and Lucy parked it in the clearing where a fitful sun was shining, doing its best to melt the hoar frost, causing it to drip off the branches of the trees. Wisps of mist were starting to rise out of the damp ground. The two women got out of the car and locked it, though heaven knows who would be about at that time in the morning in such an isolated spot and at that time of the year to try to steal it.

Looking uncertainly around Lucy decided that they would climb the bank up to the ridge, which was only about fifty feet above them, to see what they could see. They were both pleasantly warm when they reached the top, as the sun had continued to shine quite strongly out of a clear blue sky and the air was completely still.

'What are we searching for?' asked Dulcie, looking very attractive in a belted tweed overcoat and trousers tucked into what looked like flying boots with thick white woollen socks turned over the top of them. On her head was a Russian-style fur hat complete with ear muffs. She had so admired her appearance in the large cheval mirror that she had changed her mind and was now really looking forward to roaming up and over High Tor.

'I don't know,' said Lucy. 'Something unusual. Something out of place. We know for certain that something happened to them, and I think that it happened here. I don't believe in coincidences of that sort. Wrong place at the wrong time, maybe, but if I was a betting person, I would bet money on it being here. Look for evidence. Evidence of . . . devil worship . . . witchcraft . . . voodoo.'

'Voodoo?' broke in Dulcie disparagingly. 'Voodoo in England?'

Lucy raised both hands helplessly. 'There must be an explanation,' she said. 'And I know that it's to do with this place.' She started to walk along one of the narrow tracks that criss-crossed the crater. They made it to the rim at the opposite side and stared back the way that they'd come.

'It's awfully quiet up here, Lucy,' said Dulcie. 'No birds, even.'

'I expect that most of them have flown off south by now,' said Lucy, listening more intently than she had done. Yes, it was quiet, she thought. There were no whispered noises of small creatures moving. No sudden scuffles in the undergrowth. The complete lack of breeze accentuated the stillness.

They made their way further around the rim, then took another small track to cut back across the depression. Some way across, Dulcie saw something glinting at the side of the track to her left. Lucy, in front and looking the other way, had missed it. Dulcie leaned over and picked it up. A man's wristwatch. She automatically checked the time against hers. Dead right. One of those battery-operated ones.

'Lucy,' she called, holding up the watch, 'look what I've found.'

Lucy came over and took the watch. 'It's Reggie's,' she said. 'It must have come off when he was cavorting around and lost all his clothes. Never liked that metal strap. One knock and it's loose and it can fall off your wrist – not that Reggie was in any condition to notice anything like that at the time.'

She stared at the watch for a few moments and then put it in her pocket.

'It's like I said,' said Lucy. 'This is where it happened. This is where we found all his clothes, and now the watch. He wouldn't have taken his clothes off before whatever happened to him, so it must have taken place here.'

Dulcie nodded. 'Well we know that he wasn't kinky, that's for sure. Was he?' She stopped in confusion when she saw her friend's face. 'Now come on Lucy, he wasn't like that . . . was he . . . ? No . . .

I didn't think he was.' This last a little forcibly. 'So, I think you're right. Whatever happened happened here, but what can we do about it? We've found nothing out of the ordinary except his watch, and that was bound to be here somewhere, though someone coming by could have picked it up.'

Lucy stared at her friend in disbelief.

'This isn't quite what one would call a busy thoroughfare, you know, Dulcie,' she said with some acerbity.

For an hour or more they trudged back and forth across the crater. Finally they gave up and went back and sat in the car which had been warmed up inside by the sun.

'Come on,' said Lucy, 'it's no good moping about here. Let's go and see Jim Contrell and Waldorf and have a cup of tea with Sophia. I haven't had a chance to talk to her about Jim's improvement what with everything that's been going on.' She started the car, put it into gear and trundled off down the lane.

'Come in, come in,' called Jim. 'You've come to see Waldorf, have you?'

'Yes, and your mother and Len and yourself,' said Lucy. Reggie, hearing her voice, jumped to his feet and bounded out. He went to jump up on her but Jim held him off.

'Now quieten down. Remember what I told you.' Reggie, brought back to his senses by the sharp tone of Jim's voice, got down immediately with his mouth open and his tongue hanging out, wagging his tail so much that it pulled his body from side to side.

'Waldorf, Waldorf!' cried Lucy, leaning over to pat him, and he started to whimper, feeling so sorry for himself that he snuffled and cried.

'Nice old thing,' said Mrs Contrell, nodding in Reggie's direction, 'and so intelligent. Knows everything you say, don't you boy?' Reggie, unthinking, nodded his head and thumped his tail. Lucy looked at him sombrely. A little spark of recognition flashed through her head, then was gone.

Reggie went back to his thoughts. When he regained his proper self, he would make it all up to these lovely people. Why had he been so insular all these years? He had, of course, seen them and many others at Lucy's coffee evenings and 'bring and buy' sales throughout their marriage, but he had never really taken part in anything. His main effort had been to drive Lucy and her bunches of ribbons and bric-a-brac to assorted halls and country houses in the area and to take, on some occasions, three or four of the women out to various dos.

He had always been polite to Lucy's friends and anyone else, but, up till now, he had found it difficult to mix easily. He would definitely change his ways if he ever came out of this.

Lucy was speaking. 'We've been up to High Tor to see if we could find a clue as to what happened to you.' She nodded at Jim and Reggie. 'We couldn't find anything except Reggie's watch. It seems awfully quiet up there. No birds or animals about as far as we could tell. It's a pity you can't remember anything, any little snippet of a recollection that could give us some idea of what happened, because whatever it was, I'm sure it was up there at High Tor.'

Jim thought for a minute. He must not, on any account, give any indication of what was really happening. Stick to what was known, that was the ploy.

'I think that you're right, Lucy,' he said slowly. 'That's where I found myself and where Reggie and Waldorf were found, but, before that . . .' He spread his hands in a gesture of complete innocence, which was largely genuine. He still could remember nothing of his own transformation.

Lucy was looking at the watch again.

'You're lucky to have found it up there,' said Jim, 'what with all the brambles and ferns and everything.'

'Yes, we were very lucky,' said Lucy. 'As a matter of fact, that was when the idea came to me, when we were sat in the car after walking around; to clear the crater. I can get about thirty volunteers to help quite easily. It's not as though we would be cutting down mature trees or woodland, it's only ferns and brambles, and in any case, I understand that cattle get cancer of the tongue from eating ferns, so we'll be destroying a scourge in the process.'

Jim's stomach lurched. Clear the crater! Lord, no! At least not till after tomorrow.

'When were you thinking of starting?' he stuttered.

'Tomorrow,' replied Lucy. Jim blanched and started to cough to cover his confusion. 'Excuse me,' he said, reaching for his handkerchief. Reggie had also had a shock. Rising to his feet he shook his head violently and gave an ear-splitting howl which was supposed to be a 'No'.

Lucy, Dulcie, Len and Mrs Contrell backed hastily out of the kitchen, through the passage and into the front room, leaving Jim to deal with the distressed Reggie.

'There you are,' said Lucy, 'that's not the Waldorf we're used to.'

Mrs Contrell shook her head. 'First time I've seen him like that,' she said. 'It was when Jim started coughing.' She looked at Lucy. 'Perhaps he don't like people coughing?'

Lucy's eyes glittered.

'Jim started coughing and turned quite pale when I mentioned cutting down all the scrub at High Tor,' she said grimly. 'I'm sorry, Sophia, but I think that your Jim is hiding something.'

'You can't say that, Lucy,' said Mrs Contrell. 'Why should he hide anything from us?'

'Sophia . . . I don't know how to say this . . . but he's not the Jim that you are used to. That you've brought up all these years. He's really just as much a stranger to you as he is to us.' She indicated herself and Dulcie. 'He may be Jim, but not Jim as we knew him and you knew him. I can see you nodding, Len. What do you think?'

'I don't know what to think, especially now with that dog howling,' said Len. They could all hear Reggie's sobbing howls in the background and Jim going, 'Shh, Shh.' Len went on: 'That damned dog isn't normal. I remember him in the pub the other night, the first night that Jim was in there after he changed. He couldn't put enough distance between him and Jim that night. Now look at 'em, bosom pals. D'you call that normal? I don't.'

Jim had finally succeeded in calming Reggie down. 'Come on,' he said, 'now try and act normal . . . for a dog, that is.' He led him out of the kitchen and into the front room, which fell silent as they entered.

The front room wasn't very big. Come to that, the whole cottage wasn't very big, and five people and a large dog was overcrowding it to say the least. Reggie lumbered over to Lucy and put his head on her knee. He thought that his heart was about to break and moaned softly to himself. Lucy stroked his head. In his distress he stood up and put his paws on her shouders, rubbing his head against hers as he used to when they were courting and first married. 'What's going on?' she asked in wonderment of nobody in particular.

Jim said, with a new urgency in his voice, 'Come on, Waldorf, let's be 'aving you. We're going out for a walk. You've been moping about all morning.'

Lucy took hold of his paws and gently pushed him away. 'Go on,' she said, 'go on with Jim.' Jim put an arm around Reggie, pulled him into the passageway and clipped his chain on to the lead. Grabbing his parka on the way past the tiny hallstand he made his way out through the front door, dragging a protesting Reggie with him out into the lane. Once outside, the cool air seemed to pump some common sense into Reggie. He quietened down and followed Jim up the lane. Jim just kept going. He had to get away from his family and Lucy and Dulcie, as they were beginning to ask too many awkward questions.

Lucy and the others watched Jim and Reggie's hasty departure in silence. They heard the front door slam and the footsteps die away before anyone spoke. Lucy was the first.

'I'd say that those two are in cahoots, however silly that may sound. It's not like watching a man and a dog. It's like watching a team; a partnership even. That Waldorf. He's not our old, placid Waldorf. Sure, he'd bark at the postman, but he'd lick him to death once he got out. Not an ounce of bad temper in him. Never a tantrum like we've just seen. Reggie always thought that he was on the timid side, but I wouldn't like to upset this Waldorf.'

Len said, 'I did say that he had changed his attitude

towards Jim, but of course, I don't know the dog that well. You're right about him being quiet, though. Up until that last night at the pub, he was always snoozing under the benches, out of the way.'

'How's Reggie?' asked Mrs Contrell of Lucy. 'Is he getting any better?'

Lucy shook her head. 'No change except he's losing weight. They're feeding him with a drip. When I think of how Reggie used to love his food . . . it was a pleasure to cook for him. Wasn't a bit finicky. They tried to let him feed himself at the beginning, but it was no good. Nearly choked himself to death. Forgotten how to use a knife and fork. Just ate it straight off the plate. No chewing.'

'Just like a dog,' interjected Len.

'Big panic everywhere,' went on Lucy. 'They were thumping him on the back; he had a big piece of potato stuck in his windpipe and it shot out just as he was going blue in the face, and then he tried to bite everybody.'

'Just like a dog,' said Len again.

Dulcie and Lucy looked at him. A speculative look crossed Lucy's face but the thought that had caused it was immediately dismissed.

Reggie had pulled ahead and kept dragging Jim along until they reached some overhanging trees that effectively screened them from any prying eyes. Then he sank to his haunches, hung his great head and gave vent to his feelings. Huge sobs racked his body. Jim knelt down beside him, feeling uncomfortable, and reached over and hugged Reggie to him tightly. What could he say? He held the old grey dog until the sobs subsided, and Reggie pulled away from him and lay down, looking up at him with eyes full of feeling.

'Tomorrow old son, tomorrow. We'll have you there in time, so don't worry.' Jim came suddenly to a decision. 'I'll tell you what. We'll do the move today. I've got all the gear except a white coat, and I'll buy that now, when we go to town. The hospital will be pretty full. It said on the news this morning that there were a lot of people hurt in that big wind yesterday, so the place will be packed at visiting time, just as we want it to be.'

Abruptly he got to his feet.

'Let's go.' He was deliberately brusque. 'Let's do it.' And they walked purposefully up the lane to High Tor.

'We're going to go as soon as we get back to the house. If your missus has made her mind up to clear High Tor tomorrow, the news from the hospital about you vanishing will put her off – I hope,' said Jim, doing his thinking aloud. 'Another thing, they're beginning to ask too many awkward questions that I have to try to fob off without raising suspicions. That's another reason for acting now. OK? Hang on a minute, I want to make sure that your missus and Dulcie have gone, because I don't want to meet up with Mrs B-H again until all this is over.' He walked to the corner and looked down to the cottage. The car had gone.

'Come on, Reggie,' he called. 'Let's go home and have a quick snack then get going. If our luck's in, Len will be gone, down to the pub for his usual Saturday constitutional.' He lengthened his stride towards the cottage.

Chapter Fourteen

Sophia was at the sink, just finishing off the dishes when Jim and Reggie walked in.

'They've all gone then, Mam?' from Jim, more of a statement than a question.

'Yes, love. They took Len with them, he's going on to the pub. Do you want anything to eat, a cup of tea or something . . . ?'

'Yes please, Mam, a couple of quick bacon butties and then we'll be away. Got a little job to do that can't wait.' He walked to the cupboard and got out the Meaty Chunks, heaping a canful on to the tin plate with a good topping of biscuits.

'Come on, Waldorf, see this lot off. It's the last that you'll get for a bit.' He plonked it down in the back yard and went back into the house. Reggie looked after him with his heart thumping. D-day had arrived a day early. His stomach fluttered so much that he had to force himself to eat.

He looked around the yard. There was only one thing in this dog's life that he envied Waldorf: the fitness of the body he was living in at this moment.

Not much else. His viewpoint, three feet off the ground, meant that he missed a lot that he was used to. He heard Jim coming out.

''Bye, Mam. Don't wait up – we'll probably be quite late. Come on, Waldorf, we've got to get going.' He strode around to the shed at the back of the cottage and proceeded to put the horse box on to the tow hitch on the back of the tractor.

'You ride in the horse box, Reggie,' said Jim, winding up the support legs on the trailer. He opened the door set in the left front side of the box and motioned for Reggie to jump in. It wasn't dark inside as the back of the trailer was only half covered by a door that dropped down to become a ramp when the horses were loaded.

Clean straw covered the floor and the smell was quite pleasant. He scratched the straw together to make it thicker, remembering the bus journey when he had continually banged his chin. He didn't want that to happen again. He heard the tractor start up and felt it move out of the shed. There was a supermarket bag hanging up on the same hook as the bales of hay, and also some coils of thin rope. He surmised that the bag probably contained the oil and instant glue that Jim had bought, though for the life of him he couldn't figure out what on earth he was going to do with them.

The journey into town seemed endless. It was, after all, Saturday, and the traffic was heavy. They must have driven straight to the hospital, or at least to the spot quite near that Jim had previously marked out as the best place to park because, as the back was lowered and Reggie ran down the ramp, he recognised the tree-lined street they had reconnoitred what seemed an age ago.

'Come on, Reggie,' said Jim. 'Go and sit on the pavement while I uncouple this trailer and manoeuvre it into that space.'

He raised the four stabilising legs in turn and, taking the trailer off the back of the tractor, manhandled it into the kerb, pushing it as far forward as it would go. He then walked around to the back again and dropped the ramp, leaving a bare two foot between the edge where it touched the floor and the car immediately behind.

'We'll have to leave it open because if we don't some clown will park up tight behind us and we'll be in a right mess when we come bowling up here with Waldorf. Now there's a space up there where I can just fit this tractor so you wait here for me. Better still, jump in the trailer as if you're waiting for your master.' He gave a grin and jumped on the tractor and claimed his space, much to the chagrin of the man who had been waiting patiently behind him to do the same.

He walked back to Reggie.

'Now you wait here,' he said. 'I'm going to nip up town a bit quick to buy a white coat. I'll only be about twenty minutes and from here on in it will be all go so don't go on any walkabouts, d'you hear?'

Jim headed off towards the little lane at the end of the street which they had used a couple of days ago. His stomach was twittering and little shivers ran up his body. 'Concentrate, concentrate,' he ordered himself. 'What the devil are you going to be like when we really start the kidnap?' He strode on purposefully and reached the shop, was served and back at the trailer inside half an hour. Reggie sat on the ramp, whining nervously. Jim leaned over and stroked his ears.

'Don't worry, old son. It'll work, believe you me. Now I'm going to leave my watch here.' He walked into the trailer and put his watch down under the heap of straw where it wouldn't be visible to anyone just looking in. 'Three-quarters of an hour after I leave here, you must get into the hospital just as you did the other day and go through the doors of ward C straight down the corridor to the television room. When you get there, bark your head off. Right? For God's sake don't bite anyone or they will definitely want to put you down, but make as much commotion as you can. Sit in the middle of the floor and just howl. I'll only want about two minutes at the outside. Then run out back into the lift hall and down the stairs. If you see me, go a different way and give a good howl to distract attention away from me, OK? . . . I'm depending on the element of surprise. I've tried to figure it all out but . . . it's all new territory to me. And you, of course.'

He reached over and lifted down the large supermarket bag. Taking the white coat out of its wrapping, he took off all the labels and put the coat in the bag. Stepping out of the horse box with the bag in his hand, he reached over and patted Reggie.

'Don't forget. Three-quarters of an hour. Wish us luck.' Then he was gone, whistling tunelessly as he strode down the street and around the corner.

Reggie watched him go and felt dreadful. He had never consciously broken the law before. Kidnapping! A major crime. Hadn't they electrocuted somebody in the United States for that?

Meanwhile Jim had entered the hospital grounds. There were a few people about but the bulk of visitors weren't due to arrive for at least another half hour. He looked across at the porters' lodge and at the wheelchair park alongside it. There were only four wheelchairs left and not a porter in sight. They must be awfully busy. Of course, the hurricane. As casually as he could he moved across to the wheelchairs and eased one out.

In the car park he had seen an old lady being helped out of a car into a chair, and had already made up his mind that if he was queried, he would say that he was getting it for 'that old dear over there'. He pushed away up the slight hill to the path that led to the lift hall and entered it without being challenged.

He joined a small group of people waiting for lifts and when the lift arrived in he went, getting off on the third floor. He parked the chair in an alcove that held about thirty plastic chairs, reasoning that anyone wanting a wheelchair would have rung for a porter to bring one and wouldn't look for one on the third floor landing. Pushing through the doors towards ward C3 he looked down to the nurse's desk and saw that there were a few people milling around it. Three trolleys were parked in the passage with patients on them. No one took any notice of him so he pushed open Waldorf's door and went in.

Nothing seemed to have changed except that Waldorf's eyes were open. Jim went across to him and the eyes slowly focused and closed. Jim was relieved. Drugged up to the hilt. He sat down and waited for a minute in case anyone had seen him come in and was going to follow him but nobody arrived. Pulling the oil out of the bag, he went quickly over to the window shutters and ran oil on all the hinges, then put the can back in the bag. Next he produced a wooden clothes peg out of his pocket and dismantled it, putting the spring in his pocket. Taking out the tubes of glue he opened their seals and laid them ready on the side of the plastic bag. Going over to the door, he opened it and peered out, down towards the desk. Nobody so much as glanced at him. Quickly he went out into the lift hall, grabbed his wheelchair and pushed it back into Waldorf's room, his heart going like a trip hammer.

He sat down again and waited. Nothing. Getting back up he went over to the door and opened it once more, taking with him the four tubes of glue and his clothes peg pieces. He looked out. Nobody around, so he took the glue and ran it around the door where it would come up against the jamb, then, almost closing the door, he wedged the pieces of his peg under it. He was now committed. Well, might as well be hung for a sheep as a lamb. He hurried across to Waldorf and gently eased the tube out of his nose, then tackled the urine tube. His groin quivered as he looked at it. He hoped to hell that he would never have to have that indignity inflicted on himself. With a deep breath – thank God Reggie couldn't see this – he took hold of Waldorf's penis and gently eased out the tube.

The rest was fairly easy, just sensors taped on the chest and head. He pulled the wheelchair along-side the bed and put his arms around Waldorf's shoulders. He gave a heave and his heart sank. Waldorf weighed a ton. Gathering all his strength he tried again and succeeded in moving him. He had another look at the wheelchair and found that he could lift its arms out, so he removed the one nearest the bed and had another go. This time he didn't so much lift Waldorf as slide him across and on to the chair. Then he swung his legs over and, propping him up, put the arm back on. With bandages that had been used to secure Waldorf to the bed, he tied him to the wheelchair and then took a blanket off the bed and wrapped it around him. He was ready to go. Only one thing left to do: close the shutters.

He was pulling the shutters across the window when all hell broke loose. He gave a nervous grin and pulled the heavy bar in place, effectively sealing the windows from the outside. Grasping the wheelchair he pushed it to the door, opened it and looked out. Removing the pieces of peg he could hear Reggie giving the performance of his life down in the television room. He reached behind the door and pulled off the sucker with the DO NOT DISTURB notice, moistened it and stuck it on the outside of the door. He looked down the corridor towards the far end. No one was looking his way. Quickly he pushed Waldorf out into the passage and pulled the door shut behind him. Now he only hoped that that glue would live up to its promise. Instant.

Going through the double doors he went into the lift hall. He stepped into one of the big lifts that was standing open and pressed 'Ground'. The doors closed. He reached into his bag which he'd placed on Waldorf's lap, took out his white coat and quickly pulled it on, buttoning it up as the lift came to a halt and the doors opened. There were people everywhere. He pushed his way out of the lift and through a milling crowd into the hall, manoeuvring the chair into the passage against a tide of humanity, then on down the little hill and out through the gates.

Within two minutes he had reached the horse box. Getting Waldorf up the ramp nearly defeated him, but by a determined effort he finally managed it.

Giving the chair a quick shove towards the front of the trailer he applied the brakes, stepped out and raised the ramp, bolting it into place. Then, going around to the front, he opened the side door and went in and, using the thin coil of rope that he'd hung up by the hay nets, he secured the wheelchair so that it wouldn't move around when he was driving off.

Suddenly he felt shattered and sat down heavily on the floor, shaking. Kidnapping and theft. He wouldn't like to go through that again. He recovered fairly quickly and stepped out on to the road, watching for Reggie. He was taking his time. Suddenly, there he was, running like a mad thing. Jim held the door open for him and in he shot and flopped down. Jim reached in and grasped his right front leg and shook it. 'We did it, mate, we did it!' Reggie moaned and lay back on his side. He could never remember being so bushed. The relief was so great that his head ached.

Even when he was in the army he had never been involved in a riot or a civil disturbance, so the mayhem he had created as he charged into the television room barking and snarling came as a complete surprise. The terrified looks on the faces of the patients and visitors alike would haunt him for days.

He just hoped and prayed that he hadn't caused anyone a heart attack or a relapse. But they had done it. There was his human body, stuck in the wheelchair. He still couldn't work out how Jim had done it.

Jim shut the door and went to fetch the tractor, reversing it down towards the horse box. With a bit of a tussle he managed to hook it on and drove off towards the junction to make the compulsory left turn and high tail it for Merton Minor.

The traffic was very heavy and he had to wait for some considerable time before he could pull out. He looked down the road to his right – nose to tail traffic. He pulled on the hand-brake and sat back to wait, his gaze drifting across the road to the other carriageway. He caught his breath and felt his blood draining away. Lucy and Dulcie were in the outside lane with their winker going, turning towards the hospital. There was an impatient toot behind him; a car had stopped to let him out and the man behind him was probably in a hurry. He pulled out into the traffic, his mind in a whirl. He hadn't anticipated that Lucy would discover the absence of Reggie's body so quickly. What the hell could he do? There was no alternative. He had to carry on with the plan. He drove soberly along, trying not to draw undue attention to himself. His head was swimming. He trundled out of the town. A lay-by was coming up; the signs showed one-third of a mile and he decided to pull in.

He was the only one parked up. As it was a Saturday, there were no big lorries on the road, only shoppers beginning to drift home from the town and they wouldn't be stopping in any lay-by. Home for a cup of tea more like. He jumped off the tractor and opened the front door of the trailer. Reggie came up and stood by the door.

'We've got a problem, old son,' he said, stroking Reggie's ears. Reggie's expression changed; 'hang dog,' Jim thought. 'Your missus and Dulcie were turning into the hospital as we were leaving, so the muck is going to hit the fan about now.' He looked at his watch. Reggie collapsed and wobbled down against the side wall of the box and his hang dog look became more pronounced. His damned stomach began acting up again, making some weird wheezing and gurgling noises. He dived past Jim and headed for the side of the road and the hedge, where the evidence suggested that it had been used for such purposes many times before. Jim sat in the open door of the trailer and thought out loud.

'We can't go up to High Tor now . . . once they know he's gone, that will be the first place that your missus will look. She knows or thinks she knows that High Tor is the key.' He looked back in the trailer at Reggie's body, still strapped in its wheelchair, but now with its eyes open and some light starting to show in them. A funny-sounding growl issued from the lips.

'Looks like he's beginning to come round,' said Jim. 'When he's fully awake, he's going to start making a hell of a noise. It wouldn't have mattered at High Tor, but wherever we're going to hide him now we'll have to be careful. We don't want to have to gag him, but there may be no other option if we can't find somewhere secluded.' He rubbed his chin gloomily. 'Another thing, we would have left him at High Tor and gone home to make it look normal, you know, pop in for a meal and a snack and then out for a walk again as we've been doing for the last couple of days. We could have sneaked out at night when they've all gone to bed, because they sleep like the dead anyway, and gone back in the morning and they would have thought we'd got up early.'

Reggie, back from the hedge, gazed up at Jim, still gripped by panic.

'We've still got to do that,' Jim went on, 'but . . . we'll have to do it from somewhere else. But where? We'll have to move on anyway as we mustn't still be here when the posse high tails it along this road on their way up to High Tor, and they will . . . mark my words. Might be a good thing, come to that. They'll go traipsing all over the place and find zilch and we can go in there later – that's if they haven't ripped all the undergrowth off. We'll find our slot in the ground and carry on as if nothing has happened. I hope.'

He got up and motioning to Reggie said, 'Come on, in you get. We'll go on past Swiffield and try to find somewhere we can park him safely so that we can go back and establish an alibi of sorts. We'll have to bring him some food. Some of your favourite Meaty Chunks.' This with a sly chuckle at Reggie. 'Come on. Let's go.' Reggie jumped in, the door was slammed and they moved out on the road to Swiffield.

Chapter Fifteen

Lucy and Dulcie had taken nearly half an hour to park. Dulcie, driving, was in not a very good temper by the time they found a space.

'What the thump is going on?' she asked no one in particular. 'I've never known it like this.'

Lucy frowned. 'It could be that hurricane, I suppose, though I didn't think that it came up as far as this.'

They got out of the car and walked up the hill towards the alleyway leading to the lift hall. There seemed to be people everywhere. Arriving at Reggie's room, they saw the DO NOT DISTURB sign on the door. Ignoring it, they tried to go in but the door wouldn't budge. Lucy stalked off down the ward and finally managed to get to the front of a shambolic queue to question the nurse. She was met by a blank stare and a 'Come again?'

'Mr Bagshott-Hawkes's room, why is it locked with a DO NOT DISTURB sign on it?'

'Hang on a minute. I'll go and look through his records.' The nurse fingered through the files in a large cabinet behind her. 'Nothing here. Hang on another minute, I'll go and see Sister.' She picked up her book and trotted off down the corridor to one of the other wards. Five minutes later she was back with Sister in tow.

'Hello, Mrs Bagshott-Hawkes,' she said. 'I'm sorry that you've been put out, but it's probably just a precaution to stop people going in there because of the sudden rush of patients we've had, as you can see by the number of trolleys in the corridor. If you come with me . . .' Here she turned to the nurse. 'Bring your key, nurse,' and turning back to Lucy said, 'Just a precaution, as I say.' They reached the door and stood aside for the nurse to unlock it. The key clicked back and forwards, the knob turned, but they couldn't open the door.

'Perhaps it's stuck,' said Sister. 'Here, let me have a go.' It still wouldn't budge. She turned the key back and forth, back and forth. Nothing. She put her ear to the keyhole. Motioning for silence, she listened intently. She stood up and shook her head.

'Can't hear a thing,' she said. 'Nurse, get on the phone and find Dr Ramprakash. If you ladies would like to come into my office and wait – he may be a while yet, it all depends on what he's in the middle of.' She led the way to her office.

Dr Ramprakash arrived looking harassed. The situation was explained to him and he was puzzled too. He'd been in there himself that morning, and had left no instructions about locking the door. Mr Bagshott-Hawkes wasn't going anywhere.

'Could he have locked himself in?' asked Dulcie. 'We know that he isn't quite himself.' The understatement of the decade, thought Ramprakash.

He shook his head.

'That patient is so full of drugs that all he can do is lie there. And besides, there are no bolts on the other side of that door. Hospital policy, just so that this sort of thing can't happen.' He gave a tired laugh.

He spoke to the sister. 'Get a porter to climb up the fire escape outside the window and have a look in to see what's going on. Perhaps one of the storm victims has somehow managed to get in and jam the door. One thing is certain, our patient strapped to the bed hasn't done it.'

They all trooped back to Sister's office.

'Your husband?' asked Ramprakash of Dulcie. 'No.' Dulcie indicated Lucy, who leaned forward.

'He's my husband,' she said. 'Is he getting any better?'

Ramprakash looked at Lucy. 'He's no better and no worse than when he was brought in. Whatever is wrong with him doesn't seem to be progressing but then, he isn't improving either. Never had a case like it in my life before, but then I haven't been at it all that long really. I expect that in another thirty or forty years I'll have seen more cases like it and I'll be able to bore the pants off all the young doctors myself.' He gave an infectious grin.

There was a knock at the door and the porter popped his head around it, asking the sister to step outside for a minute. A few moments later Sister popped her head back inside the room and called the doctor outside. Lucy and Dulcie looked at each other. Something was up.

A muffled banging was heard just along the passage from Sister's office. The noise grew louder and louder then there was a final bang and a crash. An ominous silence descended.

Lucy got to her feet, went to the door and looked out. Two nurses and a couple of porters were peering into Reggie's room. They appeared to be searching for something. She hurried down the corridor, closely followed by Dulcie, in a complete state of bewilderment. They reached the room and practically had to force themselves into it. Ramprakash, Sister and the young nurse were in there but the bed was empty. Nobody spoke.

Ramprakash stood in the middle of the room and scratched his head.

'Should we get the police?' said Sister finally. Ramprakash threw his arms about.

'Hang about,' he said. 'There might be a simple explanation for this.' Dulcie looked at him; another Gus.

'Why are the shutters up?' she asked. They all

turned and stared at the shutters as if they had never seen any before. Sister looked at the young nurse accusingly.

'Not me, Sister,' she said. 'I've never seen them closed before. Matter of fact, I didn't even know that they were there.' She walked over and looked at them.

'There's fresh oil on them, anyway.' She touched it with her finger. 'Cor, you can smell it.'

Lucy looked at them. 'Where's Reggie?' It sounded like a wail. They all turned and looked at her.

'You don't know where he is, do you?' She was almost shouting now. 'Now come on, he must be somewhere. You can't have mislaid him. He's too big.'

A crowd had started to gather in the corridor outside the room. Ramprakash turned to Sister.

'Go back to your room and get the other doctors here. Anybody that was on this wing today. Nurse, get these people from the door and get some screens around it and none of you touch anything. Mrs Bagshott-Hawkes and your friend, could you both go back to Sister's room please. Percy,' he gestured to one of the porters, 'you stay here and don't let anyone in until you get in touch with me. Fred, you stay outside and come and get me if Perce asks you PDQ, OK?' He escorted both the women back to Sister's room.

'A cup of tea would be nice, I think. Could you

get a pot of tea in here, nurse? This could take some time.' He turned to Lucy who was close to tears. 'I'm awfully sorry about this, madam,' he said. 'I can't offer any explanation at all as yet. I think that we shall have to get the police in. We had to break the door down to get in. It wasn't locked. Looked as if it was glued shut. The bond was so strong that we had to splinter the door and jamb to gain access. And those shutters. Deliberately pulled across and secured. When I first went in I wasn't thinking straight, but there are too many strange things about that room for it to be an internal cock-up. You don't want to think "kidnap", do you, in your own hospital?'

Lucy stared at him in amazement; Dulcie's mouth hung open. Lucy gasped, 'Kidnap? What for? We haven't got anything. Who'd want to kidnap Reggie? And in that state.' She sat down suddenly. Dulcie felt unreal. This was some sort of hallucination that she was having. She'd have to phone her husband. He'd know what to do.

'Can I use your phone?' she asked.

'Certainly,' said Ramprakash, 'just dial O for an outside line.'

John was having an afternoon snack when she got through. He listened in amazement to her story and said he would get Gus if he could and bring him over as well. She rang off and looked at Lucy, who was mumbling quietly to herself.

The sister was speaking. 'That damned dog. I bet that dog had something to do with it.'

'A dog couldn't do this,' said Ramprakash forcibly.

'Dog! What dog?' demanded Lucy.

'Damned great thing. Suddenly appeared in the TV room and frightened everyone to death. Barking and howling. It was a near thing with old Mrs Gossard. Thought she was a goner. Managed to get her heart going again, though. How the Sainted Mary he got into the hospital, let alone the ward, is beyond me. Probably belongs to one of the people affected by the hurricane.'

Lucy had gone quite white.

'It's all right, Mrs Bagshott-Hawkes. He vanished as quickly as he appeared. Can I get you a chair?'

The shock's got her, thought Dulcie, and she went over to comfort her friend.

'Come on, Lucy, you've got to snap out of it,' she said, gripping Lucy's arm. Lucy shook her off. A look of comprehension appeared on her face.

'If he's not in the hospital, I know where he'll be. High Tor, that's where.' She turned to Ramprakash. 'Have they searched the rest of the hospital yet? There's no point. They won't find him, you know. This last week . . .' She collapsed into a chair crying. Dulcie stood over her with her arms around her shoulders.

Nearly an hour later she was proved right. Reggie

was not in the ward or the hospital. The police were crawling all over the room where Reggie had been and it was confirmed that a fast-acting glue had been used on the door. John Nicholas had arrived with Gus who told Lucy and Dulcie that he had no authority here as it wasn't in his police area, but that they, the local police that is, had listened with great interest to what he had to say about the recent events in Merton Minor.

The police were starting to interview the staff. To save further chaos they were allotted a room just off the lift hall to conduct their interviews. Gus was allowed to sit in and he suddenly stopped the first interview and took the officer outside.

'That's it,' he said to the young detective. 'There's your connection. That damned dog.' Gus went on to explain about Waldorf and his links with the happenings in Merton Minor. No doubt about it, the descriptions tallied. The rest of the staff had confirmed that yes, a large grey dog, obviously mad, had created hell in the recreation room and had just as suddenly vanished.

'Where did he go?' Gus wanted to know, but other than that he had run out of the ward, no one knew. Gus, going to inspect the ruins of Reggie's old room, looked around and nodded his head.

Daft Jim, it had to be. But why? He went back to the Sister's office and tossed his cap on to the desk.

'You're not going to like this,' he said to Lucy, 'but

I'm certain that all this has to do with Jim Contrell and Waldorf. That dog was here terrorising the staff and patients and I'm certain that it was when he was raising Cain in the TV room that our man was spiriting Reggie away. We can't prove it yet but I'd stake my bottom dollar on it.'

Dulcie listened in disbelief.

'Do you mean to tell us that Jim says to Waldorf, "Now listen, Waldorf, old boy, this is what you do," and Waldorf nods his wise old head and goes off and does it?'

Gus squirmed. 'What I'm saying is that Waldorf was here and lately, where Waldorf is, there you will find Jim Contrell. Also, if it was Waldorf, how did he get here, twelve miles from home? Did he walk?'

'It beggars belief,' said Dulcie. 'You've got Waldorf and Jim on the brain. While you're chasing after this figment of your vivid imagination, poor old Reggie is lost somewhere out there, and only wearing one of those hospital nightshirts. He'll be frozen to death when we find him.'

Lucy turned to her friend with some severity. 'Shut up, Dulcie. I told you that I think Jim and Waldorf are in cahoots. Gus, I'm going up to High Tor right now. Are you coming?' She got up with purpose in her manner and strode from the room. Dulcie trailed after her saying over her shoulder to her husband, 'I'm going with her. Can you come up after us? Because if we do find him, he'll probably need your services, and I'm not too happy about Lucy. She's getting some funny ideas. Was talking about voodoo and witchcraft yesterday. She'll be having a breakdown if she's not careful.'

'I'll come too,' said Gus. 'This case gets more intriguing by the minute.' They all left the hospital to return to their cars, driving off to High Tor.

The small convoy soon arrived back at Merton Minor and wound its way up past Lucy's house and the Contrells' and on up the lane to High Tor. Len, a little bleary-eyed from lunchtime in the pub, was watching the match on the box when he heard them driving past the house and looked out of the window to see the last of the cars, Gus's police car, go by. He went to the front door and looked up the lane after them.

What the devil was going on now? High Tor was becoming too popular these days. He shook his head and went back to the sport on the television.

The cars arrived at the small clearing and parked up. The men helped the women up the steep bank and when they reached the top, they stood looking around. The wind soughed through the scrub and the tall grasses rippled in waves. There was an air of desolation about the place. A rabbit scuttled out of the scrub and disappeared from view over the top of the bank opposite them. Lucy's heart sank. She had been convinced that they would find Reggie here, or at least some sign of him.

They walked around the rim, stopping every now and again to listen, but there was nothing. After some minutes of standing silently on the top Lucy turned and went back down to the cars. They all followed her.

Gus said, 'I'm going to call in to the Contrell house. There are some questions that I must put to Jim.' Sheep-like, they all got in their cars and drove down the lane.

They had a job to park all the vehicles outside Sophia's house, and the noise of the cars brought Len and Sophia to the door as they arrived at the gate.

'Is Jim in?' asked Gus from the gate.

'No,' replied Len. 'What do you want him for?'

'Few questions about Waldorf and where they've both been today.'

'He's been out since before dinner-time. Him and that blasted dog. Sorry, Mrs Bagshott-Hawkes. There's something about that animal. Mam swears that they talk to each other.'

'Any idea where they've gone?'

'Haven't the foggiest. Some garbage about doing a job for some farmer over Tetlebury way, I think. Didn't take a lot of notice. He thinks we all live in fairyland, the stories he tells us.'

'Go on,' said Gus. 'When's he coming home?'

'Not till late, according to Mam.'

'Has he got Waldorf with him?'

'Is the Pope a Catholic? 'Course he has. Some invisible umbilical cord if you ask me.'

'When he comes in, ask him to phone me. It's rather urgent.'

'Right,' said Len, then, to Lucy, 'How's the governor?'

Lucy burst into tears. Sophia hurried to the gate and the two women guided Lucy in to the cottage.

'What's happened?' said Len to Gus and John Nicholas.

'Reggie's been kidnapped from the hospital,' said Nicholas before Gus could stop him, 'and they think they saw Waldorf in the hospital when it happened.'

'Now, now, Dr Nicholas, don't jump the gun. We don't know that he's been kidnapped, we only think that it looks that way,' Gus interjected.

'And you think that Jim is mixed up in it, don't you?' said Len, not looking at all like an aggrieved brother. 'You're probably right. Wouldn't put anything past him. He's a deep 'un now. Not the old Jim. No way. You'd better come in. The kettle's on. Won't take a minute.' He led the way into the cottage.

Chapter Sixteen

The journey to Swiffield didn't take long. The entrance to the old market town was over an ancient stone bridge, hump-backed in the centre. The cattle market was on the right-hand side as they came off the bridge and Jim swung the tractor and trailer in, in a broad curve and not too fast so as not to discomfort the passengers in the trailer.

Since it wasn't market day the large area was used as a car park, but at this time on a Saturday afternoon there were more vehicles leaving than arriving. He parked and found that it was a pay and display car park, except on the stipulated market days. Taking the relevant coins from his pocket he obtained a ticket and fixed it on the windscreen then walked around to the front door of the trailer and opened it. Reggie stood up and stretched himself. Waldorf gave a low growl.

'Oh, oh,' thought Jim, 'here's where the trouble starts.' Going around to the rear of the trailer, he lowered the ramp and reached up to unstrap a large plastic curtain that rolled down to the floor and was secured by clips. He stood back and looked at it. It was almost opaque. He raised the ramp and secured it and then went back around to Reggie. Reaching back inside the horse box, he took out Waldorf's lead and shut the door then clipped the lead to Reggie's slip chain and tied the lead to the door handle. Reggie looked at him mournfully.

'It's all right, old chap. I've got to go and get some food for Waldorf and us. You stay here and guard the box and don't let anybody come near, OK? I've got to tie you up because they don't like stray dogs wandering about in a market town.'

He strode off purposefully and Reggie wriggled under the trailer to get out of the rain which had begun to fall in a fine drizzle. As the area emptied of cars it took on an air of desolation. Jim seemed to be gone for hours. The overcast sky was beginning to darken when Jim came back carrying a large plastic supermarket bag containing four tins of Meaty Chunks, a large box of dog biscuits, two big bottles of mineral water, a tin opener, a small plastic bowl, a packet containing a plastic knife, fork and spoon and a pack of cardboard picnic plates. He opened a tin of Chunks and put it on one of the cardboard plates, poured a quantity of biscuits over it and put it down by Reggie. He then unscrewed the top of the mineral water bottle and poured some of it into the bowl and put that down by Reggie too.

'Get stuck into that, my boy, and don't turn your

nose up at it. It'll do you good. I've got to try and feed your old body now, and that's probably going to be a job and a half, so you get on with that, and I'll get on with him.' So saying, he opened another tin of Meaty Chunks and put some on one of the plates, mashing it up with the plastic fork. He climbed up into the trailer with the plate of food in his hand and edged up towards Waldorf. He scooped some of the food off the plate with the spoon and held it out at arm's length. Waldorf's head came forward; hunger overcame his distrust of Jim and he gave a big sniff.

It was of course the first real food he had encountered in a week and a dribble of anticipation ran down his chin. He opened his mouth wide; Jim pushed the spoon straight in and brought it out empty. He watched in awe at the contortions on Waldorf's face as he swallowed the food. He hadn't given him much, as he knew that Waldorf's instinct to wolf the food down would result in him choking himself to death and that was the last thing they wanted.

After about the fourth spoonful, Waldorf seemed to get the hang of it but Jim thought that he had better not try him on the biscuits. After every fourth or fifth spoonful, Jim gave him a spoon of water and kept going until Waldorf turned his head away and his eyes began to close. He went out to see how Reggie was getting along.

Reggie had come to terms with life. The plate was

licked clean and the water bowl was half empty. Jim sat on the towbar and started to talk.

'I'm going to back this outfit up against the wall over there so that people can't get at the back. I know that I've curtained it off but with you tied to the front end some nosey parker could pop his head around there at the back and see what we don't want him to see.' He undid the lead and Reggie jumped into the trailer while Jim made his manoeuvres. Then he was back out tied to the door handle again.

'I'm going into town to have a meal and find a telephone,' said Jim. 'My stomach is churning, not knowing what's going on. I'd better ring Mam after I've had my meal. I'll be phoning to tell them that we're going to be later than we thought and to let her know that we're OK. But really I want to find out whether they know yet that Waldorf's gone.' He looked at his watch. 'They'll surely know by now. Your missus will have pushed it, you wait and see.' He patted Reggie's head. 'Keep your eyes open. You get back under there out of the rain, and if anyone comes near, give one of your best growls. I'll try not to be too long. So long. See you in a bit.' He walked off out of the market.

Reggie watched him go. The food had filled him with a sense of well-being but as his thoughts flickered back to what they had done today, shots of terror rippled through him. Some cars started to pull in to the car park and Reggie realised that the Saturday night revelry was getting underway as he saw the passengers spilling out, mostly young, all in good spirits. He lay still under the trailer. He wasn't going to draw any attention to himself.

Jim walked out of the marketplace and turned up the street. It was the main street, practically the only street. There were turnings off but they led mostly to dead ends. It was a typical market town street. Ironmongers, saddleries, furnishers with big chunky armchairs and settees in leather, retail arms of the cattle feed chains, outfitters displaying clothing suited to the horsy brigade.

Jim strode past looking for a pub that did meals. He stopped at the first one he saw and looked in. A bright fire burned in the grate and looking through the window into the low-ceilinged dining room he saw that it was quite full of early evening diners. He went in to the bar, ordered a pint of shandy, asked for the menu and sat down to study it at one of the highly polished dark oak tables with its red table linen and gleaming accoutrements. A smart little waitress came up to take his order and after she'd bustled off he sat there thinking.

'I wonder if they've discovered that Waldorf's gone yet? Bound to have. That Lucy wouldn't have left the hospital without seeing him.' He sipped at his shandy. He'd been dying to use the phone since they arrived in Swiffield but had put it off and put it off, through cowardice. He would phone home after he had had his meal. If it was going to be all action from then on, it would be better done on a full stomach. A sinuous squirm ran through him, leaving him feeling disjointed and unreal. He shook his head to clear it. When his meal arrived two minutes later, he didn't hurry it. He knew he was procrastinating. He looked at his watch, and decided he would phone at half past eight.

There was a telephone by the doors leading to the toilets, with cards advertising taxi services stuck on the wall around it. He got through almost immediately.

'Where are you, son?' His mother sounded worried.

'Swiffield,' he said. 'How's things, Mam? Just to tell you that I won't be home till late.'

'I think you'd better get home as quick as you can, son, there's been hell to pay here. Mr Bagshott-Hawkes has been kidnapped and they think Waldorf did it.'

'They think what?'

'Well, Waldorf is mixed up in it somehow. They were all here a couple of hours ago; a right old state Lucy was in, she had Dulcie and that doctor husband of hers with her . . . and Gus the policeman . . . They said it was definitely Waldorf.'

'But Mam, Waldorf's been with me all the time. How in the devil is he supposed to have kidnapped Mr Bagshott-Hawkes? You must have misheard it,

Mam. I'm going to phone the hospital. There must be a mistake somewhere along the line.'

'No. There's no mistake. If you'd been here you would have seen for yourself. In a terrible state they were, talking about having to break down doors and police everywhere and everybody running around like scalded cats and Waldorf going wild and biting everyone in sight. Must have been terrible, terrible.'

'But Mam, I keep telling you, Waldorf is here with me. He's been with me all day. Must be some other dog, but what was a dog doing in the hospital anyway? Shouldn't be allowed. Their own fault for letting him in . . . Where's Len? . . . Down the pub, I expect. Don't wait up, Mam. We're going to be really late.'

'Well, you take care, and you watch that Waldorf. Len says that there's something odd about that dog. He always seemed such a nice old thing to me.'

'Now, Mam. How could he harm me? I've told you that he's been with me all day, hardly out of my sight. I think I ought to ring Lucy.'

'No, don't go doing that. She's been given a sleeping tablet and ordered to bed, so you won't do any good phoning now. Better leave it till tomorrow. Goodnight, son. Take care.' She rang off.

He looked at his watch again, a quarter to nine. Just over eighteen hours to go. He walked out into the street and heard music coming from the big hotel up on the corner. He had read the notices; there was a group performing there tonight. There were quite a few young people milling about its entrance, probably from the surrounding villages. He tried to look inconspicuous.

He ambled slowly back to the car park, stopping at the entrance to read the regulations. At night it doubled as a lorry park; the motorway link road was only a couple of miles away, and all vehicles parked overnight had to be away by nine in the morning. As well as all the revellers' cars, several large articulated lorries were parked, with the curtains pulled in their sleeping compartments.

Reggie heard him coming with relief. He came out from under the trailer and stood up, giving a muted growl of welcome. Jim walked up to him and fondled his ears.

'Well, we've burned our boats now all right! They're running around back home like rats with their back-sides on fire, and *you*, they're going to shoot you on sight, I shouldn't wonder. They said that you bit people in the hospital. That's not right, is it?' Reggie shook his head frantically. 'No, I didn't think you had, but that's what they think. I don't really care what we do as long as we succeed, that is without anybody getting hurt. Breaking up some doors or windows and pinching the odd wheelchair I can handle, but nobody must get hurt . . . Well, not seriously, that is. Anything that we break or steal, you can pay for when you're back to normal, and if anybody has been traumatised you can send them on a holiday if you want. But we'll meet that situation if or when it happens.'

He went quiet, brooding, then said, 'There's no way I'm going to risk going home tonight. I think our best bet is staying here, so we'd better get in this trailer and try to get some sleep.' He leaned down and took off Reggie's lead.

'Now you slope off and get your toilet done. Don't be long.' He watched as Reggie slunk off into the darkness, then reached inside the trailer and switched on the interior light that ran off batteries. Waldorf looked at him, blinking. Opening another tin of Meaty Chunks, Jim mashed it up and fed Waldorf in the same way that he had done before. Pity he couldn't let Waldorf out the same way that he had Reggie. An offensive smell gave evidence of what would, in polite circles, be called an accident. He shook his head. There was just no way that he could envisage Waldorf excusing himself. The image of Waldorf in his present form trying to cock a leg flitted into Jim's mind and he let out an involuntary burst of laughter.

He had to do something about that smell. He rolled up the plastic and let the night air waft most of it away. He thought about Reggie when he was discovered tomorrow, back to normal. He was going to be in a right old mess. Perhaps those buggers in the space craft would clean him up, but he didn't think so. Other than switch the brains back they wouldn't do anything else. But what would Reggie feel like? He'd probably want to kill himself.

He looked over at Waldorf. Weak as a robin. No real food and no exercise for a week. He wouldn't be able to walk, much as he would want to. He would have to be found. He, Jim, would have to get people there to find him. But he was running ahead of himself. They had to get to the rendezvous first, that would be the hard bit. No matter what state they were in when they were found the whole exercise would be over as far as he was concerned, other than the telling of a few lies. He heard a scratching at the door and let Reggie in. Reggie wrinkled his nose and looked dolefully at Jim.

'I know, old son, but I don't know what to do about it. He'll just have to stay like that.' He leaned over and examined Waldorf's bonds. He busied himself taking the bindings off one at a time and retying them so that Waldorf had limited movement but would not be able to get out of the wheelchair. He stroked Waldorf's head. Waldorf accepted it and closed his eyes. 'Well,' he thought to himself, 'I've won one battle.'

The partition ran down the centre of the horse box but stopped short three feet from the back end. Its front edge was fastened to the trailer's front wall by a long piano hinge that allowed the partition to be swung from side to side. Untying the wheelchair he wheeled it around the partition at the rear and back up to the front where he secured it with the thin line again. Going back, he pulled up the pegs holding the partition to the floor and moved it over to the side that Waldorf was in, relocating the pegs in some other holes in the floor that were there for just that purpose. Anybody looking in through the front door, or over the back for that matter, would only see Jim and Reggie.

Taking down a bundle from the rack by the hay net he unrolled it to reveal a sleeping bag. It had worn-looking leather straps and was made of heavy-duty canvas. Reggie recognised it as one of the sort he had been issued with when he'd gone on army manoeuvres. They had been old then, so where the dickens had Jim got this one from? Jim was speaking again.

'Now if we do get any uninvited callers, I want you to make snuffling noises to hide any noise that he may make next door. I don't think that we shall get any, but just in case . . .' He took off his coat, and after switching off the light, wriggled into the sleeping bag. Whether he was worried or not, after two minutes Reggie heard his gentle snores. He lay on the straw thinking.

This time tomorrow it should all be over. One way or another. He prayed that nothing would go wrong, then fell fast asleep.

Chapter Seventeen

They were awake at eight-thirty. Reggie had had a foul night. Despite dropping off so quickly at first, the noise of revellers returning to their cars had woken him and he hadn't gone back to sleep properly. Jim got straight up and was busy with the sleeping bag, rolling it up and stowing it back up by the hay rack. He opened the door and glanced cautiously out. No one about, so he opened the door fully and beckoned for Reggie to venture forth to perform his toilet.

Jim, meanwhile, had opened the remaining tin of Meaty Chunks and prepared Reggie's breakfast, and was mincing up Waldorf's when Reggie came back. Reggie ate his with gusto. When he had finished it he sat back and contemplated what he had done.

'I suppose,' he thought, 'that one can acquire a taste for anything.' He turned and watched the feeding of Waldorf. He shuddered. He hoped that his body didn't develop a taste for Meaty Chunks. His imagination took hold and he could see himself and Lucy when he was back to normal.

Lucy: 'Now I've made these pasties for you, Reggie.

I've used the best Meaty Chunks that you like, and there's your jug of water.'

He quailed at the thought. His mind drifted to the hostess trolley laden with succulent goodies. Gammon, grilled tomatoes, those prize-winning sausages from the master butcher in Merton Major. His stomach gurgled and he heaved a tremendous sigh.

Jim, halfway through feeding Waldorf, looked at him curiously. 'Still hungry, old son?' Reggie shook his head wearily.

After packing the tins and plates into a plastic bag, Jim started up the tractor. 'Come on, Reggie,' he said. 'Let's make a move and get a bit nearer home before we start making definite plans. If we pull in somewhere by that golf course, we'll mull it all over and decide on a course of action.'

They took the back road to the golf course, along narrow lanes, and were roundly cursed by several drivers, held up by their slowness, who were on their way to an early round of golf. Jim grinned. He might take up the game himself. He wondered if they let you play it in prison? He drove past the golf course entrance and along to the lay-by just before the lane joined the dual-carriageway. Jim pulled in and stopped the tractor, then got off and opened the door to let Reggie out. He clipped the lead to the handle again, 'Just to be on the safe side in case there's anyone snooping about,' and proceeded to expound on what they were going to do next.

'I think that we'll start off early,' he said. 'If we go up the back by User Brook Lane, we can put this tractor in the wood by User Farm. We may be able to walk Waldorf across the fields up to High Tor. Trouble is, it's about a mile and mostly uphill, and there's no place to hide. If we're seen and challenged, it could be all up. We could take the tractor up the first part, but it's someone else's field and they may not take kindly to us roaming about over it.' He looked at his watch. Twenty past eleven. Just over three hours.

'Right! Back in the trailer, Reggie. It's getting near the wire. Wish us luck.' He solemnly leaned over and took hold of Reggie's right paw. Reggie gave a half-hearted wag of his tail. His heart was pumping so furiously that he felt he was going to have a heart attack. He turned and jumped into the horse box; Jim shut the door and drove off.

It was five past twelve when they reached the small copse of trees that Jim had mentioned. He climbed down off the tractor and listened intently. Birds twittering, the odd 'baa' of a sheep some distance away, far in the distance a train. He looked cautiously around. No sign of movement anywhere except for the animals and birds.

'Give it till quarter to one,' he thought, 'and they'll all be having Sunday lunch.' Leaving the tractor he walked on along the road looking for a gate into the field on his left. There it was, a five-barred one with a spring-loaded handle at the side of the top rail. Looking in, he saw a double track leading around the field. Good-o, they'd used tractors in there. He jumped over the gate and walked straight across the field, which was only in pasture anyway, through another gate, and rejoined the track that led over a stile and through to the field that held High Tor.

Jim sighed. Still a good three-quarters of a mile yet, but at least there were no more hedges between the stile and their destination. It would have to do. There was no more time left to formulate another plan. He hurried back to the tractor, relieved to see that there was still no one about. He checked his watch. Twenty to one, near enough.

Back at the trailer he let down the ramp and Reggie ran down. Jim went in and seized the chair; holding it steady, he steered it backwards and down the ramp.

Waldorf was swinging his head wildly around to see what was going on, making low growling noises in his throat. Jim took no notice except to snarl 'Quiet, boy' and that seemed to shut him up for a minute. Jim stood there with the wheelchair, gazing unseeingly at the tractor, working out the next step. Then abruptly he came alive. He uncoupled the horse box and drove the tractor around to where the wheelchair was. Testing the bindings on Waldorf's arms, body and legs and tilting the wheelchair backwards so that it was supported on its two main wheels, and Waldorf was lying back at an angle of some sixty degrees, he dropped the chair's handles over the back axle of the tractor and secured them with the rope out of the horse box.

Getting back on the tractor after having a last look around to see that they were still alone, he started it up again and gently eased it out of the wood on to the lane and just as gently up the road to the five-barred gate, with Waldorf howling in fear as he was trundled along backwards. Jim opened the gate wide and then drove through it.

'Go on, Reggie,' he shouted, 'close the gate. It'll catch automatically.' Reggie dutifully got on his hind legs and pushed the gate shut with a clang that assured Jim that it was well and truly shut. They repeated the procedure at the next gate and then they arrived at the stile. Jumping off the tractor Jim quickly untied the wheelchair and pushed it up to the stile.

As fast as he could, he untied Waldorf from the chair and pulled him out of it. Waldorf fell on the floor. Taking hold of the chair, Jim picked it up and flung it over the stile, then climbed over after it and hid it under the hedge. Going back over he grabbed Waldorf by the arms and attempted to pull him to his feet. Waldorf fought weakly against him. Reggie, seeing what was happening, moved in swiftly. A short bark and a quick nip of the ankle and Waldorf was weaving unsteadily on his hands and knees, leaning heavily against Jim, looking frightened to death. Jim eased him to the stile murmuring, 'Come on, boy. Come on, boy,' in his ear and Waldorf backed on to the stile, not taking his eyes off a still snarling Reggie who inched forward for every inch that Waldorf moved backwards. He fell over the stile in the end, but was too heavy for Jim to hold and slumped down on to the ground with some minor abrasions to the back of his leg. Reggie couldn't manage the stile so Jim got back over yet again and picked him up and over, dropping him next to Waldorf who cowered away from him. Picking up the bonds, they dragged Waldorf deeper into the undergrowth and lightly bound and gagged him.

'He won't move from there till we get back,' said Jim. 'We've got to get cracking and be back here by half past two to get him up and over to the place where you're going to hide. You're coming with me. Don't look at me like that; it's all part of the plan. Let's get a move on.' He picked up Reggie and tossed him back over the stile and they ran off down the hill to the tractor like a couple of kids. They picked up the trailer and turned and went back past User Farm and down User Brook Lane. Soon they were on the dual-carriageway, then at the turn off to Merton Minor and in no time at all they were pulling up at Jim's house.

He drove the tractor into the field and reversed it and the trailer into the shed, then unhitched the trailer. After switching off the tractor he went into the house. His mother was at the back door waiting for him and she went to hug him but backed away, wrinkling her nose.

'Faugh!' she said, 'where on earth have you been to pick up a smell like that? Go and wash yourself. You reek. I see that you've still got him with you.' She nodded at Reggie. 'You want to mind that he don't bite anyone.' She gave another sniff. 'You want to wash him too, he pongs a bit. Where have you both been to hum like that? And why didn't you come home last night? You had me worried.'

'Sorry, Mam. Told you, I was working, then I had a few pints and thought I'd better sleep in the trailer. Where's Len? Down the pub, I bet. He won't be back until after closing time. PG will probably have some more yarns to fill them up with.' He chuckled, hoping he was doing a good impression of nonchalant innocence, and made his way into the bathroom to try to get rid of the smell.

'You'd better wait for me outside I think, boy.' This to Reggie who was watching him to see what they were going to do next. He shouted to his mother from the bathroom. 'I'm going to nip down to Lucy's to see what the devil's been going on. I'll take Waldorf with me just for her to see that he's the same old dog she knows. Any messages?' He took off his shirt and trousers and, after emptying the pockets, nipped quickly into the shower.

'No. None that I can think of outside of what's

been going on, and I don't want to bring any of that up because seeing you there will be bad enough for her.'

'Don't be like that, Mam. I've got to go and see her. What would she think of me if she found out that I'd been home and hadn't gone down to see her, thought of that? I get on fine with Lucy.'

To say that Lucy was surprised to see them would be an understatement. Dulcie let him in. They had just finished Sunday lunch; the radio was tuned into a gardening programme. Reggie was outside. It was only when Reggie came up to him after his shower that Jim realised how much he must have ponged. Reggie smelled foul. He had kicked up a bit when they reached Lucy's house and Jim ordered him to stay outside.

Lucy looked terrible; dark rings under her eyes and a worried expression.

'Hello, Jim,' she said. 'I've been hearing some bad things about Waldorf.'

'Not true, ma'am. He's outside if you want to see him, but he smells a bit. We've been messing with cattle and I haven't had time to bath him. He's been with me all the time except when I was seeing one of the principals and he had to wait for me. Shall I bring him in? Or would you like to come out and see him?'

'No, I'll come out. Much as I want to see him, I can't have him in here if he smells that bad.' She walked to the door and opened it and Reggie jumped up to lick her face. She turned in disgust.

'Good Lord! You're right, Jim. What's he been doing? Rolling in it?'

'I think so. Dogs seem to have a penchant for that sort of thing.' He leaned over and went to rub Reggie's ears but thought better of it. 'Any news from the hospital?' he asked with a sombre look on his face.

'None at all,' said Lucy. 'It doesn't make any kind of sense. Why should anyone want to kidnap Reggie? They thought that it was you and Waldorf at first, but it's like I said to them, why would you want to do a thing like that? It's my belief that it's to do with High Tor. We went straight there after Reggie vanished last night but there was nothing up there. I really thought that we would catch them at it.'

'Who's them?' asked Jim.

'Whoever was responsible for Reggie being spirited away out of the hospital, that's who,' said Lucy.

'Look, I've got to go,' said Jim. 'Didn't realise how much he ponged till now. I'm going up to High Tor to have a look around and then come home and give him a bath if we find nothing. I'll bring him down later, when he's nice and clean.' He turned and made his way back to his mother's house.

Once there, he dug out a pair of old dungarees that had seen better days and shrugged them on. He looked at his watch – time to go. He put his head round the kitchen door and found his mother drinking tea and reading the Sunday paper. All murder and sex. A respectable woman like that reading that sort of paper? He shrugged.

'I'm popping up to High Tor, Mam. Just going to have a look around. He may be up there for all we know.'

'They all went up there last night but didn't see anything. By the way, Jim, that Gus wants to see you. Said would you pop down to see him when you came back from Swiffield. Forgot to mention it till now.'

'OK, Mam, if he rings tell him I'll be down to see him in the morning. I'm a wee bit tired today. Had a hard old day yesterday and this morning.'

Jumping on the tractor he started it up and drove out through the gate at the side of the house and up the road. Reggie trotted along behind. When they reached High Tor Jim got off the tractor to open the gate and drove in. Pointing the nose at the slope he engaged first gear. His heart was in his mouth. He let the machine tick over and edged slowly up the steep slope. Gaining the top he accelerated a little and drove straight across the crater, up the other side and down the furthest slope straight to where they had left Waldorf. He was still there.

Quickly Jim pulled the chair upright and managed to heave Waldorf into it. Looking at him Jim realised that he couldn't have lasted out much longer. He lashed the chair to the tractor again, just as he had before, and sending Reggie ahead to spy out the land drove back to the crater, stopping just above the hiding place that they had picked out. It was the work of minutes to tip Waldorf out of the chair and roll him down to the gash in the ground. Between them they dragged him into the hide and Jim checked to see that all the bonds were secure.

'OK,' he said. It's now twenty past two. I think that we should go on down the lane for a bit so that if anybody tries to come up here we can forestall them. At ten to three, no matter what, if we are with anybody, I'll say "OK, Waldorf" and you take off.' He started the tractor and trundled down the slope.

They had only reached the first bend in the road when they saw Len and Gus coming up. They were on foot but Gus was pushing his bike. As they drew near Jim stopped the engine.

'Afternoon,' he said neutrally. 'Mam tells me that you've been looking for me.'

'Yes,' said Gus, equally neutral. 'Would you mind telling me where you were yesterday afternoon between two o'clock and four?'

'Of course,' said Jim. 'I was in Swiffield with a farmer taking one of his horses to a meet. Why do you ask?'

'Was Waldorf with you?'

'Yes, but why do you want to know?'

'You and Waldorf weren't at the hospital in Merton Major yesterday, by any chance?'

'No, I was going to go but this job came up and I was stymied. Besides, Reggie is brain dead by the look of him. When I saw him the day before yesterday, he was hooked up to some machine that they said monitored brain waves and some of them weren't registering. Mam told me about that dog at the hospital biting people, but it wasn't him. Too docile for his own good, he is. And he smells. Been rolling in it.' Gus and Len nodded.

'I wondered what the smell was,' said Len. 'He wants a bath.'

'He's having one when I get him back home. OK, Waldorf.' And with those words Reggie was away, into the ditch at the side of the road, through the bushes, disappearing from sight down towards the village. The three men looked after him, Len and Gus with expressions of astonishment, Jim with a smile.

'Where the hell has he gone now?' said Gus. 'It was the word bath that got him, I think.'

'Damn,' said Jim, trying to sound convincing, 'what's got into the silly old sod now? Here, boy, here, boy,' he shouted.

The three men whistled and shouted but there was no sign of the dog. Jim got down off his tractor and went to the ditch. 'Come on, come on,' he shouted again, of course to no avail.

'He'll turn up, you'll see, like a bad penny. He'll be at our house or Lucy's I shouldn't wonder.' This from Len.

'I damn well hope so,' said Jim. 'All we need is to lose him now. Lucy would have a breakdown.'

Meanwhile Reggie had run through the ditch and across the fields parallel to the lane, initially in the opposite direction to High Tor. He loped along until he was sure that he was out of sight and then made a bee-line for the crater. He heard shouting and whistling in the distance and chuckled to himself that that Jim was putting up a good performance.

He broke through the hedge near the clearing at the top of the lane and stopped to listen. Just the normal country sounds. He looked around cautiously and, seeing that it was all clear, ran quickly across the road, crawled under the gate and gained the ridge. He stood on his hind legs and gazed alertly around, but nothing moved. He dropped back on all fours, ran to the slit in the ground and looked in.

The smell was terrible and it turned his stomach but steeling himself he attacked the thin ropes binding Waldorf with his teeth. Because, as Jim had said, each one only needed a pull on the bow knot to undo it, he soon had Waldorf free. A couple of growls and a quick nip had Waldorf crawling painfully out of the cover and sitting on the bank. Reggie climbed the bank and looked nervously around. Reason told him that there would be nobody about but the time was so near that he couldn't keep still. He lay back down and looked at his old body. What a mess.

The wheelchair was still in the bushes where Jim

had thrown it after he'd tipped Waldorf out. He would be needing that by the look of it, his poor old feet were already scratched and cut. The hospital nightshirt was in a disgusting state. When he came round he would be wearing that. His heart burned with mortification. Perhaps he could get to the brook at the side of the lane, the one that he had just run through, and clean himself up. But by the look of Waldorf, he wouldn't be able to make it to the wheelchair let alone down the hill, through the gate and down the lane.

Maybe, just maybe, it was down to Waldorf at the moment. Perhaps he didn't have the will to move himself. Perhaps when he gained occupation, he would be able to manage something. He felt his legs growing numb. He heard Waldorf making terrible noises. His last conscious thought was, 'I hope I can do something about myself before they find me.'

Chapter Eighteen

Jim, Gus and Len had given up on Waldorf and gone disconsolately home. At least, Gus and Len had, but Jim was euphoric. It was going better than he had hoped. If things went well, there would only be the problem of 'finding' Reggie and Waldorf. The sight of Reggie's body had worried him. There was a real physical weakness there. He would have to be circumspect. About eleven o'clock in the morning, he'd been told, they would be dumped back on the grass, and he reckoned they couldn't be left much longer after that. Waldorf, back in his old body, would be OK, but Reggie back in his . . . ?

It had been strapped to a bed for a week, it had had tubes stuck in it, it hadn't been fed properly and had been tied up for nearly two days. On the other hand Reggie, while in Waldorf's body, had been fully aware of what had been going on around him and the lengths to which Jim had gone to help him. Mentally, at least, he should be fine.

Jim and Len were sat in the kitchen drinking tea and looking into the fire. They had had a late dinner and Jim was wondering how he was going to tell Lucy that Waldorf had vanished. Thank God that Gus and Len were with him when Waldorf sloped off, he thought. At least she couldn't say that he had engineered that. He got up out of the comfortable old chair and went into the hall to put on his outdoor clothes.

'Where are you off to now?' said Len.

'Off down to Lucy's to try to explain how we lost Waldorf,' said Jim.

'We! Where do we get the *we* from? He just buggered off like the sort of kookie dog that he is,' said Len. The lunch-time drink was beginning to wear off. 'If you ask me, she's well shot of that dog. Ought to be put down, especially after that doing at the hospital. Yeah, yeah, yeah, I know he was with you all the time, but where were you, mister? Swiffield? Come off it. There's something going on and I only hope that you don't do anything to hurt Mam. We've looked after you all these years and never expected any thanks, only wished you could be normal, but . . . if this is normal, I'm beginning to wish that you were still the old Jim I used to look after.'

Jim felt most uncomfortable. For Len to bring up the past like that could only mean that he was worried sick. He walked across and put his hand on his brother's shoulder.

'Len. There is something going on but I can't tell you what it is. I only wish that I could. Believe me, I wouldn't do anything to hurt you or Mam. I'm going to spend the rest of my life making up to both of you for what you've done for me. Believe me, Len.' He turned and walked out of the house. Len watched him go with tears in his eyes. Then putting down his empty mug, he picked up the poker and viciously attacked the fire.

Jim strode down to Lucy's house with a confidence that he didn't feel. He walked up to her front door and rang the bell. Dulcie answered the summons.

'We've heard the bad news,' she said. 'You'd better come in, though I'd better warn you that you're not flavour of the month.'

'Who told you? Gus?' He undid his parka and was ushered into the drawing room where the imitation log fire sent out a cheery glow.

'Here's Jim come to see you, to confirm the bad news I expect. Cup of tea, Jim? We're just having one.'

He nodded. 'Yes please.' At least they weren't going to kick him out. They probably looked on him as a well-meaning bumbler. Lucy looked up.

'Hello, Jim,' she said. 'So Waldorf has run out on you too. He's probably gone looking for Reggie. Gus was sure that you were definitely mixed up in it, but when Waldorf went off and wouldn't come back, even for you, he seemed to change his mind a little. I wonder where he's gone?'

'He was heading towards Tetlebury when we saw

him last. He just took off. Gus said that my mention of a bath frightened him, but that's crazy. He'll probably be back. Either here or at Mam's house. I've shouted myself hoarse.' He stopped and sipped his tea.

'I'll have another look around in the morning, but I honestly don't know where to start. He may be back by then though. Anyway, we can't do anything now it's getting dark.'

The conversation was stilted and Jim put it down to Lucy being half drugged. Dulcie confirmed this when she saw him out.

'She's not quite with it at the moment, Jim. I'm surprised that we had that much conversation. It's the tablets. Knocking her out a bit. Goodnight, Jim. Might see you tomorrow, eh?' He said goodbye and went back home. It was way past eight o'clock and Len had buzzed off down to the pub. He went in and found his mother watching television.

'What did Lucy say?' she asked.

'Not much, she's pretty well drugged up.'

'Poor soul. I'm crying inside for her. You help her all you can, Jim. She'll need someone strong to help her through the next few weeks if they can't find Reggie.'

He poured himself a mug of tea from the ever-ready pot, put in three spoonfuls of sugar – a legacy from the old days – and sat down to watch the box. It was the first time he had been able to relax for a week.

He was in bed when Len came in. Len seemed to drink more than he used to these days. 'Probably the result of having too much time on his hands since he gave up the chore of looking after me,' thought Jim. 'When this is over, I'll help him take up a hobby of some sort.' He turned over in bed. His last thought was that he was more tired than he had realised.

Chapter Nineteen

On Monday morning Reggie awoke with a start. The sun was warm on his back and he lay there for a second or two trying to figure out where he was and how in the devil he had got there. He appeared to be lying on his stomach on the grass. He raised his head and looked around. A sense of *déjà vu* came over him, accompanied by a feeling of giddiness. Waldorf lay a few feet from him. He looked dead.

Reggie dropped his head back down on his arms as realisation came flooding back. Was it another false dawn? Were dream and reality becoming so interwoven in his head that he couldn't distinguish substance from shadow? That was Waldorf over there, wasn't it? He raised his head again, turning this way and that and his head spun and he retched. Perspiration burst from him and as he attempted to sit up the world took off on another spin. He waited for the nausea to subside and gently, so as not to cause another spasm, pushed himself into a sitting position. The events of the last few days came jangling into his head. The joy of knowing that he was Reggie again made him faint.

He looked down at himself, remembering that the last time he had seen his body it had been from the outside and it had looked a real mess, but 'mess' was too mild a word to describe the state he was in. Those damned aliens had a lot to answer for. He wondered what time it was. How long had the encounter taken? He had no recollection of the process – this time he hadn't even caught a glimpse of the alien creatures – but whatever they'd done, it had worked. He was himself again.

Lucy's image came buzzing into his mind. Her love for him, that he had seen manifested from his vantage point inside Waldorf, brought tears to his eyes. He shook himself; he was getting maudlin. He pushed himself upright with difficulty and called, 'Waldorf.' There was a faint answering twitch from the dog's body.

'Come on, boy,' said Reggie with relief. 'Come on, Waldorf.'

Waldorf sat up and looked at him, his neck stretched out, sniffing. Reggie felt acutely embarrassed.

'Waldorf, here boy.' Not a movement, just more sniffing. Reggie reached around his back and pulled at the tapes that fastened the hospital nightgown at the back. He finally managed to untie them all and slid the gown down over his arms and off. Using the unsoiled top of the nightgown, he tried to clean himself and after removing most of the loose mess he threw the gown away into the bushes. Pulling up tufts of grass, he rubbed and scrubbed until he was sore. He tried to stand up but found that he couldn't, so he turned on to his hands and knees and finally made it to the top of the ridge, which was only a few yards away but involved climbing at an angle of forty-five degrees. He rolled over and pushed himself into a sitting position, then looked around.

The wheelchair was lying in the bushes over to his right. He eased himself along, managing to reach the chair and drag it towards him. It seemed to take an age to pull it upright. Using the chair to grip on to, he finally stood on wobbly legs and took a good look around him. His chattering teeth and the ague racking his body grew worse. He turned and glanced down the slope to the road and his legs collapsed beneath him. Myra Tait and her dog were standing in the clearing at the bottom, staring up at him in silent amazement.

Chapter Twenty

Reggie's and Myra's eyes met. Reggie, in a blind panic, gave the wheelchair an involuntary push as he collapsed and it went over the edge, followed closely by Reggie, cartwheeling to the bottom of the slope and crashing against the fence with a bump that knocked the senses out of him for a minute.

Myra stood rooted to the spot. It took her some time to realise that the smelly naked man, covered with cuts and bruises, was Reggie. Reggie for his part was at the lowest ebb of his life. Tears of helplessness ran down his cheeks.

'Help me. Please help me,' he said through chattering lips.

Life returned to Myra. Quickly she ran around through the gate and knelt over him,

'My God, what happened to you?' she asked, cradling his head in her arms and trying to ignore the stench coming from him.

'I don't know,' he said, the lie coming readily to his lips, 'but if you can help me into that wheelchair, please.'

Myra tied Pug to the fence then picked up the chair that had landed nearby and placed it alongside him. Taking off her coat she draped it over his shoulders and helped him into the chair, which was a job in itself as the fall had weakened him further.

'You wait here,' she said, 'I'm going to get some help.' She turned to go.

'Don't leave me,' he pleaded, still shaking like mad. 'If you can push me down the road to Mrs Contrell's house, I'd be grateful. There's no way I'm going back to that hospital, and that's what they'll want to do with me if you go to get help. She can lend me some clothes as well, I expect, but I would like to get cleaned up before I meet Lucy.' He started to ramble and the tears of weakness started again.

Unprecedentedly, compassion gripped her. Quickly she seized the handles of the chair and pushed it over the rough ground and through the gate. Going back for Pug she tied him to the wheelchair and started off down the lane. Waldorf watched them go and slowly ambled down off the top of the ridge, following on behind.

As Myra rounded the last bend by the Contrells' cottage, she heard the tractor start up. At least one of the men was in to help her. Arriving at the cottage she left the chair outside and ran up the path to the door, hammering on the knocker. A startled Sophia answered and, taking in at a glance what was happening and the state that Reggie was in, shouted for Jim to come quick.

'We'd better get him inside before he catches pneumonia,' she said, 'if he hasn't already got it.' They had reached the door with him when Jim turned up at the end of the passage.

'My God. Reggie,' said Jim weakly.

'Quick, get on the phone to Lucy and tell her that Reggie's here,' said Sophia.

'No.' This in a gurgling voice from Reggie. 'I don't want her to see me in this state, Jim. Please help me get cleaned up before she sees me.'

Jim couldn't agree more with that sentiment. The stench emanating from Reggie was almost unbearable.

'Bring him into the bathroom,' he told them. 'You'll have to hold him up. Mam, make him a big cup of coffee with four sugars and a large whisky in it. I'll have to hold him while you wash him.' This to Myra. 'The warmth of the shower will do him good in any case.' The two women manoeuvred Reggie into the shower and he gripped the large handle screwed on to the wall. Sophia headed for the kitchen and Myra left Jim to hold Reggie while she rolled up her sleeves and turned on the shower. Taking the head off its holder, she proceeded to wash him down.

'It's the nearest that I've ever been to heaven,' Reggie thought to himself. The fact that he was as naked as the day he was born didn't worry him;

he was too far gone, and it hadn't seemed to worry the two women either. Jim and Myra made him sit down in the bath while they examined his feet, legs and arms which were bleeding from the dozen or so thorns still embedded in him.

Jim tut-tutted when he saw them. He called for the tweezers from his mother and gently pulled them out. When they finally got Reggie out of the shower, the shivering had stopped. Warm bath towels rubbed him down and after his numerous cuts and abrasions were dabbed with iodine, a pair of pyjamas was produced. Soon he was sitting in front of the fire with a warm blanket wrapped around him and the large coffee with whisky in it – or the other way round by the smell of it – in his hands.

'Right, Jim,' he said, his voice far stronger. 'You can phone Lucy now. Better tell her to bring the car and one of my suits if she would.' He gave Jim a slow grin. He was feeling better by the minute.

'Mrs Tait, I don't know how to thank you enough . . . and you, Mrs Contrell.' He sipped some more of the coffee. He was feeling light-headed, and realised that it was the whisky acting on his empty stomach. 'I'm starving,' he mumbled and in a moment Sophia was all contrition.

'I don't know what I'm thinking of,' she said. Going into the larder she took down a cake tin and picked out a rich fruit cake. She cut a hefty slice off it and put it on a plate on the arm of Reggie's chair.

'Now you put that inside you,' she said, 'and don't worry, there's heaps more where that came from.'

Dulcie took the phone call and after Jim had enquired as to how Lucy was, he asked her to bring her friend to the telephone.

'You'd better sit down, Mrs B-H,' he said slowly. 'I've got some good news for you, Reggie's here.'

He heard her gasp and then ask huskily into the mouthpiece, '*What*? Say that again.'

'Reggie's here,' he said. 'He's a bit weak but says that he doesn't want to see any doctors or anybody else, only you. He says to bring the car up and some clothes, because when he arrived here he only had his birthday suit. We've given him a bath and put a pair of Len's pyjamas on him but he'll need slippers. Waldorf's here as well, but he hasn't come into the house yet, he's still lying out in the road. You'd better get Dulcie to bring you up as you'll need help with him.' Lucy put the phone down and collapsed into the nearest chair. Dulcie looked at her with concern.

'What is it, Lucy? You look as if you've seen a ghost. Are you all right?'

'Reggie's at Sophia's house. We've got to go up and get him and take his clothes up and a pair of slippers, and socks too I shouldn't wonder. Seems that he arrived at her house completely naked.' She shuddered. What traumatic effect would that have on Reggie?

Reggie had finished the first slice of fruit cake

and was almost through the second when he felt an irresistible desire to close his eyes, if only for a second. Jim, watching him, just had time to take hold of the mug with the dregs of coffee in it as Reggie's head fell forward on to his chest. By the time Jim had lowered the back of the chair and put a cushion under his head, Reggie was sleeping the sleep of exhaustion.

That was how Lucy and Dulcie found him five minutes later. The tiny kitchen was full to bursting. Lucy went straight over to him and gave him a hug that nearly strangled him, smothering his head with kisses. Reggie didn't wake up.

'Is he all right?' she asked anxiously as Reggie continued gently snoring. 'He isn't in a coma or anything?'

'No,' said Jim, 'he's completely whacked, that's all. A good night's sleep will have him back on his feet, you'll see. And there's no need to whisper, he'd sleep through an earthquake now. Give him a week, I'd say, and he'll be back as good as new.'

Lucy turned to the assembled company. She had a job to stand up; her legs felt as though they were going to give way at any minute. Jim sprang to get her a chair.

'Can anybody tell me what happened and how you found him?'

They all started to talk at once.

Jim cut in loudly. 'It was Mrs Tait that found him.

You'd better let her tell you the story as we haven't heard it ourselves yet. Go on, Myra, tell us how you found him.'

'Well, he more or less found me, to tell you the truth. He came tumbling down the bank at the side of High Tor and virtually landed at my feet, pretty dazed because he had knocked his head against the fence in the fall.' She went on to tell all that had happened, with Jim or Sophia cutting in every now and again to clarify a point.

When the tale was finished, Jim spoke. 'I think we should get him home. He's got to go first or last so let's do it now while he's in no condition to stop us. I'll pick him up, and if you go and open the car doors, Mrs Nicholas, I'll strap him in the front seat if you can pull it back a bit. Then I'll walk Waldorf down and we can put him to bed in his own house. When he wakes up he'll feel much better being in familiar surroundings.'

Everybody started moving at once. It had only taken a little bit of a firm voice to motivate them. Getting Reggie home worked like clockwork. Inside half an hour, he was tucked up in his own bed for the first time since the previous Friday night.

Waldorf was allowed in to the conservatory and fed a bowl of his old Meaty Chunks, then he went and flopped in Reggie's armchair. Nobody had the heart to scoot him out of it. Dulcie and Lucy had a chat and Dulcie decided that she would stay the night but first she phoned her husband to tell him what had happened. He wanted to hot-foot it over there to get all the details but she told him that she would pop back home briefly to check that everything was all right and give him the full story. She put the phone down and went back upstairs to tell Lucy what was going on and found her sitting by the bed holding Reggie's hand.

'I'm going now, dear,' Dulcie whispered. 'Be back in an hour. It'll take me half that time to tell him what's happened. Wants to know the ins and outs of everything, but I suppose I would be the same if I heard about this second hand. Even though I was there, I still can't make head or tail of it!'

She went downstairs and out through the front door, slamming it shut behind her. Lucy heard her go and the house was quiet. She looked at Reggie, sleeping like a baby. A sort of reality had returned.

She supposed that a doctor would have to see Reggie. She supposed that the police would be around trying to figure out how he had been abducted from the hospital and arrived at High Tor. They could all wait. He was going to have a good night's sleep and *nobody* was going to be allowed to disturb him. She put his arm back under the bedclothes and, closing the curtains, left the room. Absently patting Waldorf as she went by him into the kitchen, she reached over and took the phone off the hook. She made herself a pot of tea and settled down to wait for Dulcie.

Epilogue

Friday night, the eighth of October 1992, and the pub was packed. Reggie was standing at the bar. His mind drifted back five years. Funny how his life had changed since then. He now had more friends than he had ever had before. He had taken to being an active member of the community and had found that the more you do for others, the more people want to do for you. Most nights, when he came into the pub, people came up to him for a chat but tonight he had fended them off, as he was waiting for Wharfman's new general manager, a bright young man who had taken the company by its ears and pulled it screaming into the twentieth century.

Reggie had developed a new zest for life. A 'let's get at it' attitude that rubbed off on his staff. They'd also noticed a subtle change in his manner, which was not anywhere near as abrasive as it had used to be.

'It was that brush with death that changed him,' was the general verdict.

Waldorf, asleep under the bench as usual, had also

changed. Five human years is about thirty-five in dog years.

'A pensioner,' thought Reggie. Guard dog par excellence. Waldorf also had a new bed. Reggie had given him his favourite armchair and he was allowed to sleep in it in the lounge, except when they had visitors. Then he would, in fine weather, be tied up to the garage by the water butt.

Lucy had seen Reggie, on more than one occasion, leaning with his hand resting on the rim of the said butt, looking down into the water and chuckling to himself. She would ask, 'What are you laughing at, Reggie?' but he would just shake his head and walk away, still chortling.

Myra Tait and her husband Stan had become firm friends of theirs and Myra had asked, quite innocently, albeit with a twinkle in her eye, on more than one occasion, 'Let's see more of you in future.' At those moments he had felt quite a reprobate, remembering what he had done to poor old Pug. He had bought a new collar for Pug, but the little dog never ever came into the garden these days.

Gus had given up trying to solve the case. He had had the wheelchair thoroughly examined but it didn't reveal any clues. He had looked at Waldorf and wished that he could talk.

Reggie couldn't remember anything, so he said, except snippets about a bearded gypsy type with a scruffy dog, something like Waldorf, vaguely in the back of his memory. This was said with tongue so firmly in cheek that it was a wonder that the words came out. No mention of 'blobs' or spaceships. He had decided to tell no one the truth about what happened, not even Lucy – he didn't want to be branded a madman. All that mattered was that everything was back to normal.

The nine-day wonder ran its course and, as the saying goes about ill winds, in his case it had done rather a lot of good. In fact it was more like a sea change in his life. He stood at the bar, contentment oozing through him, and saw his visitor come in through the pub door and approach him, calling out to the regulars as he did so.

'Evening, Reggie,' he said, when he finally reached the counter. 'Can I get you another drink?'

'Certainly, Jim,' said Reggie. 'I'll have another gin and tonic.'